Wishful think

"You look like a

colored bulbs hanging all over you."

He yanked her downward, and she fell in a heap beside him. The ground's dampness seeped through her overalls while the smell of wet grass filled each breath. Several paint balls whizzed over them, hitting a tree. "Those were meant for us," he whispered.

His gaze fixed on hers and neither moved. Whether a second or several minutes passed, she had no idea. His smoldering eyes sent her heart pounding, and her mouth went dry. He hesitantly touched her face, running the tips of his fingers over her high cheekbone. His tenderness sent an ache through her, an ache for him to care about her the same way she'd begun caring for him.

He plucked a twig from her hair and tossed it aside. Entwining his fingers in her hair, he began closing the inches separating them. With every fiber of her being, she longed for his kiss, but at what cost? So she could cry herself to sleep every night when he replaced her with his American dream?

Kinsy forced herself to break the spell he'd unknowingly cast over them. She rose up on an elbow and aimed for a lightness she was miles from capturing. "The gallant knight routine again, huh?"

"Yes." He brushed the dirt of her cheek. "My poor, distressed damsel."

She replayed his words. *My poor distressed damsel.* He'd said *my* not *the* or *a*, but he called her his. *I'm overreacting and having a bout of wishful dreaming.*

JERI ODELL is a native of Tucson, Arizona. She has been married over twenty-five years and has three adult children. Jeri holds family dear to her heart, second only to God. *Remnant of Victory* is Jeri's first full-length novel and she is thanking God for the privilege of writing for Him. When not writing or reading, she teaches a college girls' Sunday school class and leads a mid-week Bible study for them. Jeri is also attempting to scrapbook twenty years worth of family photos—a major feat!

Remnant of Victory

Jeri Odell

Heartsong Presents

With deep gratitude to my friend and editor Deborah White Smith and with deeper gratitude to my Lord and Savior, Jesus Christ.

A note from the author:
I love to hear from my readers! You may correspond with me by writing:

Jeri Odell
Author Relations
PO Box 719
Uhrichsville, OH 44683

ISBN 1-58660-152-0

REMNANT OF VICTORY

Cover design by Robyn Martins

PRINTED IN THE U.S.A.

prologue

Vietnam 1974

“Mama, Thai and I are going out to play.” Loi said to their tiny, almond-eyed mother.

Bending down, Mama hugged Thai. Her long black hair fell forward and tickled his cheek. He loved the way she smelled like fresh flowers. Then lifting Loi’s chin, she said, “You behave and avoid trouble. Watch out for Thai.”

Loi nodded. “Of course, Mama.” He wrapped his skinny arms around their mother’s tiny waist for a quick hug before he ran out the door.

Four-year old Thai followed his older brother into the sunshine of a brand new day. In his haste to keep up, he slammed the door of the small room they rented. He chased after Loi who, at six, was Thai’s hero. Thai considered him to be a man of courage, curiosity, and imagination. Cautious, Thai dreamed of being more like Loi.

The scent of the wet grass beneath his sandals filled the air, and Thai sucked in a deep breath. With Loi as his leader, life resembled one big adventure, unless Mama found out. Trailing behind Loi toward the Saigon River, they probably faced another day of mischief. Then the adventures would end because they’d be forced to stay indoors for their disobedience.

They scurried through the crowded streets. Thai and Loi counted the soldiers they passed on their journey to the river. Thai couldn't count past ten, so he started over several times. The military was as much a part of their lives as the sun rising and lighting up the deep blue sky each morning. In Saigon, uniformed men walking around town was normal. Thai knew no other way of life.

When they arrived at the river, the boys found a spot to sit on a sandy bank and watch the boats come and go. The sand stuck to the back of Thai's bare legs, making them itch. "I don't like the war," Thai said as he brushed sand off the back of his knobby knee. "The killing makes me afraid."

"You're a baby. Nothing but a baby. I'm not afraid of a thing," Loi said, puffing out his chest.

"I am not a baby! Mama says I'll grow big someday, and she says being afraid is okay. She's scared, too, sometimes." After all, they'd lost most of the people they loved because of this war, including Daddy.

"Mama said the war and its dangers are a long way off from Saigon," Loi reminded him.

His statement seemed true enough. Constant gunshots no longer echoed around them.

"She says most of these city dwellers have never seen or heard the war. That's why she moved us here, remember?" Loi spoke with absolute certainty.

Thai nodded. He missed the small fishing village they'd once called home; he longed for the family they'd once lived with. Now there were only the three of them. Everyone else had died: their grandmother, grandfather, two uncles, and their families. Just like Daddy, they were all gone because of the stupid old war.

A few of the American solders—the ones with the tan uniforms—came over and asked the boys to play kick the can. Thai kicked off his sandals, and the warm sand squeezed between his toes. He played hard, trying to keep up with Loi. When the soldiers returned to work, Loi and Thai walked along the riverbank. The water surged by in a noisy and powerful display. Thai stayed several feet away from the edge while Loi tempted fate and walked mere inches from the precipice.

Loi's eyes sparkled. "I like the soldiers. I'm going to be a soldier too when I'm old enough. I'll march and carry a gun just like Daddy used to."

Thai hoped he was never old enough. He didn't voice the thought because Loi would again call him a baby.

On the walk to their mother's flower cart to get their lunch, Loi ducked through a rough district. Goosebumps trickled along the back of Thai's neck. He disliked going this way, so he ran to catch up with Loi's longer, faster stride. But Thai wasn't fast enough. Someone grabbed him from behind and pulled him into a back alley. A large hand covered his mouth, and he gagged against the smell of sweat mingled with dirt. Loi kept going, never realizing that Thai no longer followed.

"I have a present for you, little boy," the uniformed Vietnamese soldier whispered. Though Thai could understand the man's Vietnamese, he talked slightly different than the people Thai knew. "Was your daddy a soldier?"

Thai nodded. His heart thumped in his chest. He struggled to breathe with the large palm covering most of his face.

"I won't hurt you," the man assured him. "If you promise not to scream, I'll remove my hand. I have a present from your daddy."

Thai nodded his agreement, and the large hand dropped from his face to a vise grip on his arm.

"He asked me to give you this." The man pulled out a small red item from his pocket. Thai had never seen anything like it before. When the man pushed a button, fire shot out. He patiently showed Thai how to operate the lighter, as he dubbed the red object. Thai relaxed, realizing this man offered friendship.

"The red one is mine," the man said. "This blue one is for you. Don't use the lighter until you have many people around to see the present. The fire might only work once." Thai nodded his understanding. "Go." Then he waved his hand toward the street, "And remember, save the lighter until you can share the fire with lots of people."

Thai ran from the alley gently cradling the present in his hands. *A gift from Daddy! A gift from Daddy!* As he rushed toward his mama's cart, the chant bubbled within him. Desperately, Thai hoped to catch up with Loi before he arrived alone. They'd both be in trouble if Loi got back without him. He spotted his brother sitting on the curb about a block from the cart.

Excited, Thai showed Loi his surprise. He demonstrated how to press the button without actually pushing down. Thai explained about the soldier who knew their daddy. Clutching his hand tightly around the treasure, he said, "I'm saving the present to surprise Mama someday when she's sad."

Just as he began slipping the lighter into his pocket, Loi grabbed the prize. He raced off, leaving a sobbing Thai in his wake. When Thai rounded the corner, he caught a glimpse of Loi standing near Mama on the sidewalk, next to her flower cart. Then several pedestrians blocked them from his view.

Thai ran around them and spotted Loi as he held up the

lighter. "No! It's mine. It's mine," he screamed. "That's not fair! I'm supposed to show her!"

Loi glanced his direction.

Thai yelled again. "Mama, don't let him push the button. That's my surprise—"

A flash of light preceded the explosion. The flower cart splintered into fiery pieces of debris. Thai fell to the ground. The unyielding sidewalk tore into his knees and palms. The screams of pedestrians crashed against his ears. Fire and smoke blocked all sight of Mama or Loi.

"No!" Thai screamed as sobs racked his body and a cloak of desolation covered his soul.

one

Thai parked his white Mazda Miata curbside in front of a sprawling brick home in an older Pasadena neighborhood. He double checked the address and hopped out. A manicured lawn caught his attention. Only in California. Back home, in Illinois, nothing green grew in January.

A basketball hoop hanging above the garage and a wide sidewalk winding through the neighborhood suggested that this house was the perfect place for a kid to grow up. Pastor McCoy's raising seven children here underscored the truth. He'd told Thai that afternoon during the job interview that all seven were girls. He'd also offered Thai the position of College Minister at Christ Community Church.

Thai rang the doorbell and watched two neighbor girls bicycle by. Their giggles and chatter drew a smile. He glanced at the cloudless sky. In his hometown, warm days like this didn't happen until late spring. Life in California looked promising.

"Hello, you must be Thai," a lilting voice greeted him.

He turned back to the doorway. A pair of chestnut brown, almond eyes welcomed him. His breath caught in his throat. His heart pounded. His nightmare from last night returned. Four-year-old Thai stood in Saigon, looking at his mother for the last time. Visions of the explosion filled his mind.

"Are you all right?" Her brows drew together.

He swallowed hard, forcing himself back to the present. "I'm fine. Is this the McCoy residence?"

"Yes." She smiled, extending her hand in a friendly gesture. He forced himself to offer the same courtesy, taking her small, soft hand in his. "I'm Kinsy, Karl's second daughter. Come in. The family is expecting you." He followed her petite frame—clad in jeans and a sweatshirt—through a tiled entry hall and into a large family room where Karl watched a UCLA basketball game on a big-screen TV.

Karl rose and shook his hand. His gray, thinning hair added to his distinguished appearance. "Thai, welcome. Did you meet Kinsy?" Karl smiled proudly at his petite Asian daughter and Thai nodded. "You'll meet the rest of the crew at dinner. Do you like basketball?"

"Very much, Sir."

"Then join me for the end of the game. Only five minutes left, and don't be so formal. Call me Karl. The rest of the staff does." His warm blue eyes offered friendship.

Thai joined Karl on the large taupe sectional, made to accommodate a dozen or so people. Kinsy took the cushion next to his, and he caught a whiff of apple blossoms. He tried to focus on the game, but ended up wondering about Kinsy instead. *Was Karl's wife Asian? Maybe he'd served in the war and married a Vietnamese woman. God, what are you doing to me?* The farther Thai tried to run from his Vietnamese roots, God seemed to keep bringing him full circle. Would he ever succeed in his goal to bury the past and forever forget?

During a commercial, Karl informed him, "Kinsy is on staff at Christ Community, too. You'll work together a lot, I'm sure. She's the Missions Director and worked closely with our last college minister." Thai's heart plummeted farther. She'd be a constant part of his ministry here, making her hard to avoid.

"College kids are the most eager and available for short term missions work." Kinsy grinned, and her amiable overtures both repelled and attracted him. "Of course you know the facts."

"Mission trips are a large part of my ministry philosophy," Thai said. "I like to see the kids involved and growing in service. I find that, while serving, many of them realize their gifts and God-given potential." Thai wasn't going to let one little woman with a gumdrop nose steal this chance at his dream job. Known as a cutting-edge church, he'd desired to serve on staff at Christ Community since his seminary days in Dallas. Somehow, he'd avoid Kinsy and tolerate her—and the memories she resurrected—only when he had to.

"I agree." Her hundred-watt smile shined upon him. "On a mission trip in eighth grade to Sells, Arizona, I led several of the Indian children to the Lord. The experience changed my life. I knew I didn't want a day to go by that I didn't share Christ's love with someone." Her eyes danced with a passion for God.

"That's my girl," Karl declared. "Her heart's desire is for all to know Him."

"Someday, I hope to return to Vietnam, find my birth mother's people, and tell them about Jesus." Her words resonated with a longing ache.

The statement also answered his question about her parentage. She must be adopted.

"Have you ever been back?" she asked.

"No." He paused, wondering how much he should reveal.

"I have no plans to return, ever."

Her eyes rounded, but she didn't miss a beat. "I do. I long to see my mother's homeland, learn of their customs, embrace my heritage." Yet her steady gaze asked, *How can you not long for the same*? "I don't remember Vietnam," she continued. "I was adopted as a baby. Do you—"

"Too well, Kinsy. I remember too well."

"Dinner's ready," Mrs. McCoy called from the hallway as the tantalizing smells encouraged ready response. Relieved by her impeccable timing, Thai rose.

Karl flicked off the TV and led the way to the dining room where a long cherry-wood table dominated the room. "Thai, this is my wife Kettie and our two youngest daughters Kamie and Kelsy."

"Good to meet you ladies." Kettie looked remarkably young for having daughters as old as she did. The only signs of age were telltale crow's feet fanning out from her brown eyes as she smiled. Kelsy had her father's blue eyes and looked just like him. Kamie, also Asian, wore her hair long and straight, and Thai recalled that last morning when his mother's long hair tickled his face.

"Smells delicious." He tried to sound normal, but the memory unsettled him. His hand automatically went to his cheek. "I haven't had a home cooked meal in a while."

"Excuse the huge table," Kettie said. "We just gather at one end rather than removing the leaf. I never know when all the girls will be home, or when we'll have company." Thai noted at least a dozen chairs flanking the table. Then the plump roast caught his eye, sitting on a platter like a king surrounded by the rest of the feast. His stomach growled, and he hoped no one noticed.

Karl took the seat at the end, and Kettie claimed the chair to his right. He motioned Thai to the place on his left. Kinsy sat next to Thai, and the other two girls seized the chairs beside their mom. When Kinsy reached for his hand, he jumped. *What is she doing?* Then Karl clasped his other hand and started praying. Thai expelled a long slow breath.

For a second, he wondered if the pastor's daughter was making a play for him. She was pretty, intelligent, but Asian. If she weren't Asian, he wouldn't have minded holding her hand. She possessed what he most admired in a woman: a fervor for evangelism. But she also represented what he most wanted to avoid: Vietnamese roots. As her fingers moved in his, Thai determined all the more to forget Vietnam or die trying.

❧

Kinsy passed Thai the mashed potatoes and wondered about the horror on his face when he met her. Maybe she'd caught him off guard. After all, he'd faced the street when she'd opened the door. And who, after meeting her blue-eyed, fair-skinned dad, would expect an Amerasian daughter?

But somehow she knew that her nationality didn't just surprise him. Kinsy spooned gravy onto her potatoes and continued unraveling the mystery. Again, Thai had looked uncomfortable when he met Kamie. The two of them seemed to trigger unpleasant memories from his distant past. And she'd never forget the pain in his voice when he vowed never to return to their shared birthplace. His reasons for not wanting to go back plagued Kinsy.

"Thai, tell us about your American family," her mom encouraged in a warm, interested tone. She sipped her iced tea and waited expectantly.

A tender smile touched his lips as his brown eyes softened. Kinsy admired his high cheekbones and thick midnight black hair. "My dad was a lifer in the Air Force. He served in Vietnam, and God gave him a compassion for the people and their plight. When he returned after the war, he and his wife adopted Tong and me."

Thai paused and cut off a bite of his roast. "This is delicious—tender and juicy."

"Mom's a great cook," Kelsy bragged.

"How old is Tong?" Kettie continued in the tone her daughter deemed interrogation, but Thai seemed comfortable with the questions.

"He's twenty-eight. Two years younger than me." He buttered his roll.

"Same age as Kinsy," her mother observed. "Is he a blood relative?"

"No."

Kinsy hoped Thai might share more, but he didn't.

"Where are you from?" Kinsy asked.

"Chicago area."

"My sister Kally went to school at Trinity. She's a teacher."

Thai nodded. "I went to Wheaton."

"Kylie, another sister almost went there," Kelsy informed him. "Then she decided to buck tradition and go to a state school."

"How in the world do you keep track of all these K's?" Thai asked with a chuckle. "Do all seven of you have names beginning with K?"

"Karly, Kinsy, Kally, Korby, Kylie, Kamie, Kelsy," all three sisters recited at once.

"Don't worry, you're certainly not the first to be confused," Karl assured him. "Seemed the thing to do at the time, since Kettie and I are also K's, but I think we've regretted the decision more than once." He paused and lifted a forkful of mashed potatoes to his mouth. "Did your parents have any biological children?"

"Three, but they are much older than Tong and me. My parents were around forty-five when they adopted us, so they are well into their seventies now."

"Healthy, I hope," Karl said while slicing off another piece of roast. He offered Thai a slice, which he gladly accepted.

"Yes, thank the Lord. Dad retired from the military about fifteen years ago, and, once Tong and I finished college, they started traveling in an RV. They have a ministry of sorts, holding Bible studies in each campground they visit. They've led countless elderly people to the Lord." He looked at Kinsy. "They share your passion for the lost."

Since first meeting at the front door, he'd avoided direct eye contact with her—until now. Her heart did this crazy little flip-flop, sending electricity clear to her toes. His ebony eyes reminded her of chips of coal, and, in their depths, deep wounds smoldered.

"Anyway, they're happy." He turned back toward her parents. "I'm sure they'll pop up here one day soon. They have to make sure I'm fine and check out the new church where I'm serving. You know how that is."

Both Karl and Kettie nodded. "You bet we do," they said in unison.

❧

Dinner conversation continued to comfortably flow until the meal's end. As everyone stood, Thai expressed his thanks. "The meal was beyond wonderful, Kettie. Let me help clean up."

"Traditionally, we play a game of basketball to decide who gets the honor," Karl informed him.

"But first we put the food away," Kettie reminded. "So if everyone will grab a dish. . ."

Thai carried the mashed potato and gravy bowls into a large country kitchen decorated in blue checks. In no time, the perishables were covered and stored in the refrigerator, and everyone headed out front for the game.

They played several games of Rock, Paper, and Scissors to choose the team captains. Kinsy and Kettie won the honors.

"Karl," Kettie said without hesitation.

"Thai," Kinsy called. Then Kettie took Kelsy, and Kamie joined their team.

Asian versus non-Asian, Thai thought. Of course, he found himself stuck with the two he least desired to team up with.

Since Kettie picked the first player, Kinsy's team started with the ball. Kamie threw it in, and Kinsy gracefully headed for the basket. Karl blocked her shot, spun around, and shot for two.

Kamie tossed the ball to him this time, and he dribbled to the basket. Karl planted himself in Thai's path, so he passed the ball to Kinsy. Open, she took the shot. "Two-two." She grinned and gave him a high five.

Thai really got into the game. Both he and Kinsy were competitive, so they made great partners. In a short amount of time, they left the other team behind. Thai admired her courage on the court—a little hundred-pound dynamo, energetic and fearless.

"Looks like Kettie, Kelsy, and I have dish duty," Karl announced through puffs of breath. "You two won't be on the same team again." He grinned at Thai and Kinsy.

I hope you're right.

Kinsy gave Thai one last high five.

"Dad, don't forget I need a ride home," Kinsy said.

Two little frown lines marred the space between Kettie's two perfectly arched eyebrows. "Where's your car?"

"In the shop. Dad brought me home from work with him."

"Thai, would you mind dropping Kinsy off? Her apartment is near where you're staying."

His fists clenched. *I'd rather not.* "Sure, but my offer for cleanup still stands."

"Absolutely not," Karl declared. "You won—fair and square. No dish duty tonight."

"Okay. Thanks for everything—the job, the dinner, and the fun." Thai shook Karl's and then Kettie's hand.

"Our pleasure," Karl assured him. "I always like to have new staff over to get acquainted with my family and vice versa."

"Well, thank you. I had a good time." He turned to Kinsy. "You ready?"

"I'll grab my things and be right out." She hugged her dad, mom, and sisters, dashed into the house, and returned a minute later with her purse and briefcase.

Once they were inside the car, Thai asked, "Where to?" He started the engine, turned on the lights, and pulled away from the curb.

"Hop on the 210 and head east. Do you know how to get to 210?"

He nodded. Somewhere deep inside, he acknowledged she was the cutest, perkiest, most fascinating woman he'd met in ages. She loved God, played basketball like a guy, and her eyes—warm pools of melted chocolate—invited him to wade on in. After a few minutes of quiet, Thai searched for something to say. "I liked your family."

"Aren't they wonderful?" Her tone reflected a smile of approval and pride. "I was so blessed. My growing up years were great. Not perfect—but filled with love."

"I feel the same way about my American parents." His home had been filled with love, too, but the pain of his early years always overshadowed the present. He didn't want to remember his mom and Loi, yet their memories wove themselves around him like a second skin. "Did you like growing up in a large family?" he asked, ready to voyage into any realm of small talk to avoid his past.

"I did. We had fun, crazy, frustrating and maddening times. I will tell you this, I plan to have at least four kids, maybe as many as eight. Some will be adopted, of course."

"Of course. I have the same goal to adopt, but eight kids? I hope your future fellow's desires match yours." He wondered if she had a special guy in her life. *Why do I care? She's Asian!*

"He will, or he won't be my future fellow. Kids are very important to me. Some things in life are non-negotiable. Take the next exit and go left."

"What else is non-negotiable?" He glanced at her pretty profile, barely visible through evening's shadows.

"I only have three—Christ, kids, and cherished."

"Only three? Makes you pretty low maintenance," he teased. Her light tone put him at ease, and Thai enjoyed their easy banter. "Christ and kids are pretty self-explanatory, but cherished?"

"Right at the light. My dad," her voice took on a dream-like quality, "says God created all women to be cherished, adored, and loved beyond belief. I won't settle for less.

Neither will my sisters."

In the dark, with no reminder of her Asian heritage, he longed to be the man who'd cherish her. Different from most girls he'd met—she seemed open and real. She stirred something within him—his own yearning to be loved and cherished.

"Pull over by the curb. This is my complex. Thanks for the ride, Thai. See you at work tomorrow."

Wishing the evening didn't have to end, he considered walking her to the door, but then the dome light illuminated the car. He looked into her almond eyes. Oh those eyes. . . just like mother's. . . Her cropped hair gleamed in the limited light, indicating that it was as silky as his mom's. Thai touched his cheek. Instead of offering to escort her, he bid her an abrupt good night and drove off into the darkness.

two

Kinsy watched Thai pull away from the curb and drive from her peaceful, tree-lined neighborhood. Heading upstairs to her apartment, she unlocked the front door. Kally, her next-youngest sister, sat cross-legged on the couch, grading papers. "Hey, Kal." Kinsy hung her purse and briefcase on the hall tree. "How come you didn't come for dinner tonight? Did you get my message?" She plopped down in a matching blue plaid armchair.

"Yeah, I did, but Danielle made pasta, so I stuck around here. I needed to do laundry and get these reports graded."

"I figured she did. The garlic and onion met me about halfway up the steps." Should she say anything about Thai? Dying to talk the situation through with somebody, she plunged in. "I met a guy. . ."

She now had Kally's full attention. "The new college minister?"

Kinsy nodded. "Something about him really intrigues me. Problem is something about me apparently repulses him."

"Oh, come on."

"No, I'm serious. I saw the dislike in his eyes. He's also Vietnamese. I wonder if he's prejudiced against his own people. He reacted oddly to both Kamie and me."

"Why are you intrigued then?"

"I'm not sure. He's very good looking for one thing," she joked.

"Kinsy, you've never been swayed by looks."

"No, but they don't hurt." She grinned. "I'd like to know what makes him tick. Sounds rather corny, but he seems like this great guy with some big, hidden secret. I'd like to solve the puzzle."

"Always love a challenge, don't you?" Kally's dark eyebrow shot up, daring her to deny the truth.

She didn't bother. "I don't understand. How can he not yearn to know about his homeland? Why isn't he at least curious about his Asian heritage?"

Kally watched with those intense brown eyes of hers. Her hair and eyes were the darkest of all the McCoy's natural children.

Kinsy paced between the living room and dining room. "Kamie and I ache to know more about Vietnam. Why wouldn't he?"

"At what age was he adopted?" Kally set her students' reports aside and stretched.

"Six, I think Dad said."

"Maybe he remembers things he'd just as soon forget. Those six years must have been right smack in the middle of the Vietnam War. He would have been affected just like all the American soldiers who fought there."

Kinsy spun around to face her sister. "I bet you're right! You just solved the mystery of Thai Leopold. Maybe that's why he gets a haunted look on his face whenever he sees Kamie or me. Tonight in the car—surrounded by darkness—he acted more relaxed. When I opened the door and the light came on, he turned cold as ice." She returned to her favorite spot in the house, the old, worn armchair. Plopping down, she dangled her feet and legs over one arm.

"He probably lived through some horrible atrocities of war," Kally said. "No wonder he has no desire to return.

You don't remember Vietnam. He probably can't forget."

"You know, he said something about remembering too well. I wonder how can I help him?"

"Pray for God to bring healing. And maybe the kindest thing you can do is stay away from him."

"Yeah, like that's an option. We're going to be working side by side." Besides, Kinsy didn't want to stay away, but deep inside she knew her sister had a point. If she caused him pain, what kind of friend would she be to keep hanging around? "I will pray for him." She raise her chin with determination. "A lot."

Kinsy wandered into the kitchen and poured herself some water. "I know!" Taking a sip of the cold liquid, she continued, "The Bible smuggling trip I'm working on for the college kids may be to 'Nam. He probably just needs to face his skeletons."

Kally came around the corner. "You'd better pray about this first. If looking at you and Kamie is difficult, I don't think forcing the poor guy on a trip is the answer."

"Don't you think God brought him here for a reason?"

"Absolutely," her sister assured her. "But you just met the guy, for Pete's sake, and God may not have brought him here for your reason. Only God can change him, Kinsy. You can't."

"I know, but God can use me in the process."

"Slow down. That's all I'm asking. You know how you tend to plow ahead under your own steam."

Kinsy nodded. Kally was right. Sometimes she struggled to discern whether God led her or if she'd run a mile ahead of Him. Her tendency to jump in and get things done often got her into trouble.

"I'll be careful and prayerful, I promise." She hugged

her sister. "I think I'll turn in."

" 'Night, Kins. I'll pray, too."

After she readied for bed, Kinsy read a Psalm and a chapter of Proverbs, part of her nightly routine. Then she prayed for Thai. "I don't know what Thai needs, but You do. Touch him, Father, please." She lay awake for a long time, thinking about a man she barely knew. A man she hoped to help.

❧

Thai tossed his keys on the hotel dresser. Hating the stuffy smell of hotel rooms, he opened the window. The church had rented him the moderate room while he visited L.A. for his interviews. Now the job officially belonged to him, so he'd have to find a place to live. As he moved toward the bed, Thai noticed the message light blinking on his phone, and the red flash blurred into images of a grenade's blowing up his grandparents' home. He balled his fists and shoved the images to the back of his mind.

Hand shaking, Thai hit the message light. After listening to his brother's voice, he punched in the frequently dialed the number.

"Hey, Tong," Thai said, reclining against the headboard of the queen-size bed.

"I called to congratulate you, but you don't sound like a man who just landed his dream job. What gives? Your voice is dragging the ground like a worm's belly."

"I don't know. Maybe I made a mistake. Maybe this isn't God's plan for me."

"What are you talking about?" Tong exclaimed. "This position has been your prayer for six years."

"I don't know. I'm just having some doubts, I guess."

"Isn't that normal? I felt the same when I got on the

force. Don't you remember? And you told me that when I had prayed about something that long that the open door just had to be God."

Thai sighed and ran his hand through his hair and grimaced at his brother's use of his own words against him. "Yeah, I remember."

"What gives? Don't you like Pastor McCoy?"

"Very much. He's as warm and gracious in person as he is in his books. He took me home for dinner to meet the fam."

"So, why the doubts? Didn't like his wife, family, other staff members, what?" Tong released his battery of questions with his usual determination to get to the bottom of every case.

"Kinsy and Kamie—his daughters. They're Vietnamese."

"Oh." Tong's quiet response echoed with understanding. They'd shared a lifetime of confidences, friendship, and respect.

"Every time I looked at Kinsy, all I could see was my mother dying in the explosion. She's just another reminder that I'm to blame."

"Thai, that explosion—it. . .it wasn't your fault."

"I just need to forget. How can I do that here? Kinsy is on the church staff. The Mission's Director! We'll end up working together on a couple of projects a year. There's no possible way to avoid her."

"God knew all this before He led you there," Tong assured.

A twist of irritation slithered through Thai's midsection. He didn't want answers, just someone to listen. "How are Lola and the kids?"

"Fine. We're planning a trip this summer to visit you and Mickey Mouse."

If I'm still here. "Ah, I get the picture. Living near Disneyland is an asset to draw visitors. I figure Mom and Dad will be here in the next few months."

"You figure right. They're headed west, and I'm sure you're a bigger draw than even old Mickey. I don't blame them for not hanging around here in the winter, but we sure miss them. Hang on a second. . . . Night, Hon. I'll be there in a minute. Okay. . .Lola sends her love."

"And I send mine. You're sure a lucky man." A touch of envy crept into Thai's heart. "You have a nice life and a great wife. I wouldn't mind meeting a little blond dream like Lola."

"Why does she have to be blond, Thai? Maybe God has a brunette for you. Maybe God has an Asian wife for you." The hint of impatience rising in Tong's voice reflected their previous discussions on this very topic. In a heated conversation, Tong even accused his older brother of putting limits on God.

"You don't remember Vietnam, but I do, and I want to forget." Thai snapped. "Part of my plan to leave the past behind is to marry American. If she's blond, all the better.

"Remember when I was in junior high and the kids called me names?" Thai continued. "I promised myself right then that no kid of mine would live through any of those experiences. When I met Tyler Evans, I knew I'd found my answer. Even though he was half Asian, no one teased him because he looked like a blond California kid with a great tan."

"You know, God has used Lola's nightmare for his glory," Tong said as if Thai's argument meant nothing. "Maybe He can do the same for you,"

"I don't know. . ."

"Neither did she, but look how God has used her rape to help others find healing. It's really weird, but I met her because she was raped. Don't you see how different her life would be if she hid from her past?"

"But—"

"She often says, 'Only God can take our tragedies and make them triumphs.' I'm not denying that you haven't had your share of tragedy, but. . ."

Thai let out a long, slow breath and ran his hand through his hair. "I can't make any promises right now. Just pray for me—tons."

Tong chuckled. "I will, big brother. Uh. . .so, care to tell me about Kinsy McCoy?"

"Not really."

"Don't sound so threatened."

Thai sat up on the edge of the bed and untied his shoes. "I never said I was threatened. I've only met her once, and just spent this evening with her."

"And?"

"She seems terrific. Okay, maybe more terrific than anyone I've met in a long time, but—"

"But?"

"She's Vietnamese, man, I already told you."

"And her nationality supersedes everything?"

"For me, yes."

"Is she beautiful?"

"Umm."

"Love the Lord?"

"Passionately."

"So God has brought you to a new church where there is a beautiful, terrific, in-love-with-God woman, and you're complaining?"

"Things aren't so simple."

"I know, Thai." Tong sighed. "Lola went through a lot after her experience. I just wish you could—"

"You don't wish half as much as I do." Thai rubbed the base of his neck.

"Do you mind if I share this with Lola? I think it's time the two of us change our praying for you."

He gripped the receiver. Was Tong right? He'd spent the last twenty-six years running from memories. *I think I need help, Lord. Enable me to look at Kinsy without the painful flashbacks. I'm so weary.*

"Thai?"

"Yes. That's fine. Go ahead and share with Lola."

"Thanks, and hey, enjoy your first day of work tomorrow."

"I'll try. . .I'll try."

"I love ya, Bro."

"Me, too."

❧

Later in the night, Thai awoke, yelling, "No!" He sat up, drenched in sweat. His heart pounded. His gulped in air as if he'd jogged several miles. The explosion mixed with terrified screaming reverberated through his mind.

Thai turned on the hotel lamp and grabbed his Bible. He'd read a few Psalms to temporarily erase the memory. He'd killed his mother and brother, and the guilt weighed heavier in the night than at any other time.

The words blurred. Thai closed his eyes, seeing fire and smoke. The scent of burning flesh smelled as real as it had twenty-six years ago. The shrieks of horror rang in his ears. Visions of people running in every direction, yet going nowhere.

Thai lay in a crumpled mass of misery on an unyielding

sidewalk. "Mama, Mama," he screamed over and over, but she didn't answer or come to him. People yelling, children crying, women screaming, and sirens rang out around him, but he dared not open his eyes, afraid of what he might see.

He lay with his knees curled under him, his face buried in his forearms, his side pressed tightly against a building. Continual sobs racked his thin body. Smelling the smoke, he wondered if the fire would get him. Taking a deep breath, he forced himself to raise his head just a little. He peered through one squinted eye toward Mama's flower cart. Gone, and in its place laid pieces of charred debris.

"Mama," he screamed again. Then he caught a glimpse of her, recognizing a torn piece of her bright pink dress. Two men loaded her tiny frame onto a stretcher. He ran to her. "Mama, Mama." His little hand reached for her, but she didn't reach back. He touched her stiff, still hand, and he knew Mama was dead, gone just like daddy.

A piercing scream wrenched itself from the center of Thai's being. He held tight to Mama's hand.

"Somebody get this kid out of the way!" A soldier yelled, trying to maneuver the stretcher into an ambulance.

Another soldier lifted Thai by his upper arm, carrying him several feet away, and unceremoniously plunking him down. "Get lost kid."

Frantically, he searched for Loi, spotting his brother's unmoving body against the curb. A melted piece of the blue lighter lay mere inches from his arm. One of the soldiers picked it up. He smelled it. "The kid blew the place up with a V.C. lighter."

"They trick kids with these all the time," the man who'd moved Thai said, shaking his head.

More screams tore from Thai. His surprise killed Mama and Loi. His entire body shook from the force of his pain.

Finally, a man standing nearby yelled at him. "Shut up, boy! Just shut up!"

But Thai couldn't stop. His agony, too deep, too real, poured out in louder wails.

The man walked over to him, grabbed him, and shook him until Thai thought his teeth would fall out. "I'm sick of your noise. I said stop!"

Thai bit his lip. His loud weeping turned to silent sobs.

"Leave him alone!" someone warned in broken Vietnamese. Thai recognized Sarge, one of the American soldiers who played with him and Loi down near the river. He lifted Thai into his arms. "Tell old Sarge what's the matter with his little buddy."

Thai pointed to Loi's lifeless body and the weeping broke out again. Sarge hugged Thai close and let him cry. He patted his back and whispered soft words near Thai's ear. Though Thai didn't understand the meaning of the English words, he understood the comfort Sarge offered.

When Thai's screams quieted to hiccupping sobs, Sarge asked about his family. Thai told him they were all dead. Sarge's eyes teared up, and he hugged Thai tighter. "I'll take you to the American orphanage. They'll care for you well," Sarge promised.

three

Two and a half months had passed since Thai joined the staff at Christ Community, and Kinsy evaded him day after day. After more of Tong's coercing, Thai promised his brother and himself that he wouldn't avoid her. Therefore, her avoiding him proved bewildering, with a twist of ironic humor.

She came to meetings late and left early. No matter where he sat, she chose the opposite side of the room. Whenever he almost passed her in a hall, she ducked into someone's office or into a restroom. CC—a church with a staff of over fifty—had his and Kinsy's offices in separate corridors, making eluding him easy for her. But why did she, and why did he care?

In truth, something about the greatly respected woman fascinated him. Her avoiding him only heightened the fascination. The staff sang her praises. She did her job well. Kinsy was almost perfect. Her only visible flaw, her nationality, even seemed less important.

Thai had been praying a lot, spending extra time in the Word. Now stronger, and ready to test his strength, he wondered how he could with Kinsy avoiding him. He'd been learning to take captive his thoughts and tell himself the truth. Kinsy looked nothing like his mother, except her eyes. Looking at her didn't have to trigger a reaction.

Today, during their regular Wednesday chapel service and staff meeting, he planned to corner her about the

Bible smuggling trip she planned for the college group. April lingered only a week away; time to get moving on details. She'd sent out promo material, but the destination remained unknown.

Thai waited at the chapel entrance, next to the double wooden doors with the stained glass crosses embedded in them. Chapel service had started about five minutes before, and the staff's voices rang out in a chorus of "I Love You Lord." Kinsy rounded the corner, stopping abruptly. She wore a navy blue suit, and the tailored lines showed off her tiny waist.

"Thai." She recovered quickly. "How are you? I haven't seen you in ages."

Of course you haven't, because you're avoiding me like a bad disease. "I'm well. How about yourself?" He leaned on the chapel door, crossing his arms. Inwardly, he dared her to ditch him this time. She stopped in front of him. They stared at one another for a second. His mother's face flashed before him. The explosion came next. Thai stopped the resulting flinch. *I can do this, in Your strength.* He blinked and focused on Kinsy.

"I'm fine, too," she said. "We'd better go in. We're already late."

He straightened. "Mind if I sit with you?"

Her mouth fell open. "Not at all."

❧

Thai held the door open for Kinsy and followed her to a row near the back. She tried to focus on the praise and worship but struggled to forget the man standing next to her. She closed her eyes, enjoying his rich tenor voice, wrapping around her like a warm blanket.

Kinsy attempted to listen to her father's teaching as he

continued leading them through a study on the book of Isaiah. Her confused mind kept thinking about Thai. She'd taken Kally's advice, and for his sake, avoided him. And Kinsy had prayed faithfully and daily for him. Now, he sought her out.

The college kids were already his fans, including her two youngest sisters. Most of the girls considered him cute, and the guys labeled him cool. Her dad referred to Thai as a gifted Bible teacher. Nobody had to convince her. Somehow her heart knew that wonderful described him adequately, but he still had problems that Kinsy seemed to increase. She tried not to take offense, although she couldn't deny the pain in his eyes just moments ago.

He passed her a note. *Can we have lunch*?

She smiled. A bubble of hope rose within her. God must be answering her prayers. *When?* she scribbled back. *And why?* she wondered.

"As soon as we're through here," he whispered, looking right at her.

Today he wore his wire-rimmed glasses, and he looked as good in them as he did in contacts. His striped dress shirt and blue tie looked casual with the sleeves rolled up a couple of folds. Something about the way he gazed at her made her heart almost forget to beat. "Sure." But she wondered if going was the smart thing to do since she already liked him too much for her own good.

As soon as the meeting ended, Thai swept her away to Baja Fresh, a little Mexican restaurant that smelled like fajita heaven. "Hope you like this place," he said, as they stepped toward the line.

"One of my favorites."

"Mine, too. I discovered this one on my second day of

work. I come here like three times a week. We never had Mexican food like this in Chicago."

"Exactly what Kally said."

After they ordered, he led her to a corner table. "What other culinary treasures have you discovered?" she asked.

He still avoided eye contact with her most of the time, fixing his gaze on his drink. "In and Out Burger and California Pizza Kitchen. My other two hangouts."

"To cover the other four days of the week?" she teased.

"Just about. I don't cook much, but I sure appreciate your mom's occasional invitations. Hers are the only three home cooked meals I've had since I got here."

"How pathetic." She wondered if he was hinting for an invitation from her.

He cleared his throat. "Have I offended you?" Now he looked directly at her with an intensity that bore into her soul.

Kinsy choked on her soda. "What?"

"You've avoided me since the night we met. I wondered why."

"Number 74," the counter help called out.

"Excuse me." Thai went to claim their order.

Oh, great. Thanks, Kally! Now what do I say? she stormed. *The truth. The truth is always good.* Kally's voice echoed in her head.

Thai returned, placing Kinsy's burrito in front of her. She fingered the paper wrapper, hoping Thai had forgotten his question.

"So, what gives?" he asked. "Am I imagining things or have you spent the last two months running from me?"

Kinsy tore the burrito's wrapper. Taking a deep breath, she blurted out, "Yes, but my sister told me to."

"Your sister told you to avoid me?" He cocked one

eyebrow, challenging her to convince him. "Which sister?"

"Kally."

He wrinkled his forehead. "Kally? Kally doesn't even know me. We've never even met." He flung up his hand.

"I told her about meeting you and how uncomfortable you seemed around Kamie and me. She figured your reaction has something to do with your past in Vietnam." The smell of grilled onions and peppers wafted around her.

"I didn't realize I was so obvious." He sipped his soda as if he were trying to swallow a lump in his throat.

"Seemed to hurt you to look at either of us, so Kally said the kindest thing I could do was stay out of your way. And I've really tried."

"I'm sorry, Kinsy. Don't take my problem personally. It's just that. . .when I look at you, I remember things I've tried a lifetime to forget." His face tightened into a mask of anguish.

She nodded her understanding, and her throat constricted. "Don't worry, Thai. I've gotten good at staying out of your way." She made a weak attempt at a joke. "We don't have to spend time together."

The slight smile suggested that he appreciated her sensitivity. "The problem is my brother says we do."

"Your brother?"

"He thinks the time has come for me to quit running from the past."

"Sounds like we have a face off between my sister and your brother."

Thai chuckled and unwrapped his burrito. "He thinks practice makes perfect and the more time I spend with you, the easier being around you will get."

"So you expect me to ignore Kally?" Kinsy chided.

"She'll not appreciate your brother taking precedence over her." Not sure she liked Tong's prescription, Kinsy excused herself and went to the salsa bar.

The problem was that spending time with him put her heart in danger, more than ignoring him did. During the past two months, the more she avoided him, the more she yearned to stop avoiding him. Everything about him—even his painful past—appealed to her. Developing a friendship, opening her heart to him, placed Kinsy in risky waters.

His cautious eyes suggested that Thai only needed her help to get over his past. No promise of a relationship or hope of commitment lingered in their inky depths. Was she willing to play the guinea pig in his experiment?

Kinsy settled at the table with several types of salsa she didn't even remember dishing up.

"Let's pray," Thai said.

Without thinking, Kinsy reached for his hand. A spark ignited at their touch. His startled gaze preceded a stiff prayer. By the time he tacked on the amen, her hand felt singed.

She busied herself with her lunch, hoping Thai didn't recognize the attraction she knew must be pathetically displayed all over her face. She noticed his questioning gaze in her peripheral vision, but didn't look up.

❧

Thai returned to their previous conversation. Anything to take his mind off the 110 volts that had just passed between them. "So what do you say to Tong's plan?"

She hesitated. Probably thinking the whole idea was insane—just as he did. But he'd promised Tong he'd at least try.

"I'm not asking you to be my best friend, Kinsy," Thai

assured.

"Well, what a relief," she said flippantly, "since I already have one. I don't think Danielle would appreciate your usurping her spot."

"I promise, I'm no threat to Danielle. Will you just quit avoiding me? Maybe we can share an occasional lunch."

She hesitated again. "Sure—I guess."

He didn't understand the tinge of distrust in her voice, and they finished their lunch in silence.

"March in L.A. is great," he commented on their way back to the car, hoping to regain the easy camaraderie they had shared briefly in the restaurant. "No snow to shovel, no coats, no boots."

"Just a warm breeze," Kinsy said. He opened her door, and she slipped into his leather seat.

On the drive back to the church, Thai concentrated on the passing hotels, restaurants, and various businesses. What could he say now since he'd accomplished his mission? Finally, he grasped at a new topic. "So tell me about this big staff retreat coming up in a couple of weeks. The one everybody's talking about."

"Once a year in April, the whole staff goes to Yosemite for five days. We stay at Emerald Cove near Bass Lake. The whole point of the trip is to build unity and refresh us spiritually. Each year, we take a new trail. This year the plan is conquering Half Dome. Have you ever been to Yosemite?"

"No."

"I don't think there's a prettier place this side of heaven. Do you like to hike?"

"I'm not an avid hiker, but I enjoy hitting the trail occasionally."

"Me, too," she admitted.

"I do enjoy the outdoors and nature. Your dad said this year's theme is team building."

"Yeah. His goal is for those of us who work together on a regular basis to strengthen our bonds, thereby strengthening our ministries. My guess is you'll be teamed up with the youth ministry leaders."

"How about you?"

"I'm not sure where he'll put me. Maybe with you guys. I work with the college, high school, and junior high ministries a lot."

He hoped not. An occasional lunch was one thing, spending a week together seemed a little more than he desired to tackle. At once, his friendly overtures mocked him. He planned to call the shots—spend time with her on his terms, when he so desired. Now, he wondered if Tong was right. Maybe God had other plans. Thai again fought an urge to run from Kinsy—far and fast.

"I think they are posting the list today. Shall we check?" she asked when they pulled into the church parking lot. "The trip is only a couple of weeks away."

Thai and Kinsy made their way to the office bulletin board behind the receptionist's desk. "Hello, Sally," they both chimed in unison. She nodded, busy answering a call.

Kinsy spotted their team first. "Looks like Tong's getting his wish. We are on the same team."

Thai nodded, but didn't say anything. He and Kinsy were paired with Chris and Rob, the high school and junior high ministers. Four people made up each team. Talk about intimacy. Dread rose like bile in his throat. His newfound strength vanished like a sand castle whisked away by the tide. Had anything really changed inside of him?

"Thanks for lunch," Kinsy said, glancing at her watch. "I've got to run. I'll see you around." She started to walk away, but stopped. "And no ducking," she whispered and winked. Then she was gone.

Trouble, no doubt. She sent his heart reeling in two directions. Half of him really liked her and liked the idea of spending time together. The other half hated looking into those eyes. . . . He glanced back at the team list and sighed. Tong had been praying again.

❧

"I remind him of something or someone he's been trying for years to forget." Kinsy informed Kally and Danielle at dinner. Aimlessly, she pushed the peas around her plate. "The problem is he reminds me of someone I hope never to forget."

"You've got it bad, girl." Danielle grinned and took a sip of milk.

"I do." Kinsy groaned, taking a bite of rice. "I've got a major crush on a guy who can barely stand to look at me. Now I have to spend a week with him. The teams will do everything together, from the time they get up until lights out."

"Gives you about seventy-five hours to win his heart." Kally informed her in her no-nonsense schoolteacher voice.

"No hope there. His goal is to tolerate being around me, not fall for me." Kinsy pushed her half-eaten dinner away, no longer hungry. The smell of the grilled chicken didn't even tempt her. "To make matters worse, the Bible smuggling trip this summer looks more and more like we'll head to Vietnam. He'll hate me if that happens."

"Kinsy!" Kally's exasperation rang through loud and clear. "I told you not to manipulate the situation."

"I didn't. Honest. At least not completely. There were four places open last fall when we applied, and I told Steve to pray about where to send us. I said our team would go anywhere, but picked Vietnam as our first choice. I never retracted the request, even after learning of Thai's aversion. As Steve and I both prayed, the Lord is closing doors elsewhere and flinging them open for 'Nam."

"Who's Steve?" Danielle asked.

"He organizes the trips."

"I sure hope you're hearing God and not your own will," Kally said. Sometimes her to-the-point personality irked Kinsy.

"You apparently have your doubts." Kinsy's annoyance laced the clipped accusation.

"Well, you have been known to jump the gun."

"Kally, I really care about Thai. I don't want to hurt him. Believe me, at this point I'm begging God to send us anywhere but Vietnam. I'm sure—just like you—Thai will assume I manipulated the whole thing." *Then I'd never stand a chance with him—never. Not that I really do now!*

"So when will you know?" Kally's tone now held a trace of sympathy.

"Not until May. I'm sure Steve will know before then, but they don't like the teams to have too much advance notice. Security and all."

❧

Thai hadn't spent time with Kinsy since their lunch two weeks before. He'd passed her in the hall twice, and she didn't run the other direction. She actually smiled and said hello. They'd exchanged E-mails about the upcoming Bible smuggling trip, but no personal contact.

Monday morning—retreat day—showed up right on schedule and proved to be another warm L.A. day. Thai donned a pair of khakis and his favorite Chicago Bears T-shirt. He sighed on his way out of his apartment. From now until late Friday evening, he and Kinsy were expected to be connected at the elbow. If he could erase her disturbing presence from the equation, a great trip awaited him.

As he pulled into the church parking lot, he spotted Kinsy unloading a sleeping bag from the trunk of her frog-green Del Sol. She bounced over and deposited her bag in the pile with about twenty others. Perky. The word described her from the tip of her short molasses-colored hair to the toes of her white Nikes. Petite. Perky. Asian.

Thai parked his car and unloaded his own things. About half the staff had already arrived. With a grumbling engine protesting all the way, a rented bus pulled into the parking lot. The hissing brakes brought the beast to a halt. Diesel fumes filled the air, and Thai wrinkled his nose.

He and a few others helped the driver load everything in the storage area under the bus. Then Karl called the staff together for prayer. After praying, he said, "Let's load up. Pretend you're Siamese quadruplets for the next five days."

Chris and Rob were the first two on the bus, so they claimed the back seat. Thai settled next to them. Kinsy boarded almost last. Thai watched her come down the aisle all smiles and sunshine. She wore a pair of jean shorts and a pink T-shirt. Emotions warred within. He was simultaneously torn between his attraction to her and a need to run from her.

Their gazes met when she was halfway to the back of the bus. She paused for a microsecond, as if to tenderly say, *I know this is hard for you.* Like one of those slow motion commercials, he sat mesmerized as a beautiful girl moved toward him. Their gaze lengthened, and he didn't have the willpower to look away.

Kinsy smiled—just for him. Thai discovered a growing fondness for her smile, and he grinned back at her. She stopped in front of Thai, Chris, and Rob and peered at the three of them. "Don't the bad boys ride in the back of the bus?" she asked with a lifted brow.

"You got it, babe." Rob grabbed her wrist and pulled her down on the seat between him and Thai. "And you're our bad girl for the week," he teased.

A twinge of jealousy shot through Thai.

Kinsy stood up and faced Rob with hands on hips. "I'm nobody's babe, bad or otherwise. Understood, buster?" she joked, poking him in the chest with her index finger.

"I like a woman with spirit," Rob countered, grabbing the offending finger.

"Too bad, she said she'd be my woman this week," Chris informed them, winking at Kinsy.

"Fellows, fellows. You'll have to share. Now who will let me have a window seat?" She batted her eyelashes.

Thai rose, and she slid in next to him. Both Chris and Rob complained.

"I know a gentleman when I see one," Kinsy informed them. "Now, you two need to practice losing gracefully and quit your bellyaching." She faced the window, ending the conversation.

After the bus started rolling, Kinsy leaned toward Thai and quietly said, "I wasn't sure you'd want me this close."

Part of me does—more than you could ever know. "I figured I'd better protect you from the sharks," Thai quipped.

"Well thank you, gallant knight."

"My pleasure, damsel in distress."

Thai wondered if Kinsy had ever dated either one of those two; both were flirty and familiar. *But I shouldn't care*. Nonetheless, Thai did care.

"I'm not getting in the middle of something, am I?" Thai asked a few minutes later.

"What do you mean?"

"Rob seems interested."

Kinsy laughed. "Rob flirts with anything female. He's definitely not my type."

"So what *is* your type, Miss McCoy?"

"Tender, sensitive. You know."

"Why are all women looking for a sensitive man?"

She giggled, reminding him of tinkling bells.

"I don't know," she said. "But I guess most of us are."

"Do you have a boyfriend?"

"No. Haven't for years."

Why did those words please him? She was not at all what he was looking for. At least not the outer package. "Your mom said you're twenty-eight. How many years could it have been?"

"I'm embarrassed to tell you. Way too long. How about you? Anyone waiting in the wings?"

"You're not fooling me with the old bait and switch tactic. You tell me how long, then we'll talk about my pathetic love life."

"Sounds promising. Here's the deal. I fell in love briefly my freshman year of college. For about ten minutes, I thought he might be the one. For right now, God's plan seems to be singleness."

"Are you fine with that?"

"Most of the time, at least until my younger sister—four years younger, mind you—got married last year. Suddenly, I felt like an old spinster."

"Which sister?"

"Korby."

"Is she the only one who's married?"

"Yes."

"Where does she fall in the lineup?"

"Fourth. Just after Kally. Now, your turn to spill the beans."

"I've never been in love. Dated lots of women, but can't ever seem to get past the third date."

"Three strikes and they're out?"

"Yeah, I guess. By then I always know they aren't the one woman I'm looking for."

"And what will she be like—that one woman?"

"She'll love God, me, and life." He realized he'd just described Kinsy, except the "love him" part. "And she'll be blond."

"Blond?" Kinsy frowned. "Oh—as far from Asian as possible?"

He nodded. "Yep."

Kinsy squinted, then turned to gaze at the passing California countryside. Although the sun brushed the plowed fields around Fresno with sparkling diamonds of light, the brightness faded from his day. Why did he make the blond comment just when they were enjoying each other? Was it a reminder to him or to her?

Neither spoke the rest of the trip. Thai recognized the resemblance between the barren plowed earth lying just past the freeway and his own life. Both appeared bleak, empty, and filled with deep ruts. A little boy with a life just as bleak, just as empty, surfaced.

The American orphanage loomed at the end of the driveway like an imposing gray monster. The old three-story building appeared cold and uninviting. Thai wrapped his arms tighter around Sarge's neck where he sat on his lap in the passenger seat of the camouflage-colored jeep.

They bounced along the rutted drive, dust billowing behind them. The jeep rolled to a stop near the front door. Sarge carried Thai into the front office where a stern, red-headed woman with a tight bun typed on an old machine.

Sarge spoke to her in English. Thai knew by Sarge's compassionate tone and his frequent glances toward Thai that he told her about Mama. The woman's face remained professional, unmoved. Fear gripped Thai. This didn't seem like a nice place. No one would love him here.

Sarge picked up Thai. "This is good-bye, little buddy. You be a good boy for old Sarge."

Tears pricked Thai's eyes. He held tight to Sarge. The strong man buried his head against Thai's bony shoulder. His body shook, and Thai pleaded, "Can't you keep me?"

Sarge raised his head, his red, tear-filled eyes begging for Thai's understanding. "I wish I could little buddy, but the army won't let me. I'll try and come back for a visit, though. I've got to go now."

He tried to place Thai on the floor, but Thai held tight to his neck. Sarge pried Thai's little hands loose, but he only grabbed hold again. Finally, the woman held on to Thai while Sarge left. Sarge turned and waved, tears running down the big man's face. He said something, but Thai couldn't hear the words because of his own wails.

When the woman finally let him go, Thai ran out the door to where the jeep had been. It was gone. Only the dust of departure remained. Thai ran up the long driveway until his legs would go no farther. At last, he collapsed on the dirt drive, a rock digging into his knee. He lay in the dirt and sobbed until someone carried him back to the orphanage.

four

Kinsy didn't turn toward Thai or invite conversation again. His blond comment hurt. Just another reminder she'd never be anything more than someone he was learning to tolerate as a means of overcoming his past. She refused to let his subtle rejection ruin this trip. *I'll show you, Thai Leopold! You'll never meet a blond like me, and it'll be your loss.*

As the bus groaned up the last steep hill, camp waited right around the bend. Kinsy said a quick prayer, sucked in a deep breath, and decided to forget Thai's mindset toward her. She'd be charming, friendly, and as normal as she could manage. He'd not put a damper on her mood or her hopes.

The bus squealed to a halt. The staff, chatting and laughing, crowded into the aisles. Since they were in the back, Kinsy and Thai were the last two off the bus. She stopped just before exiting and turned to him. "The first thing you should do is take a huge sniff of this mountain air. Nothing like the stuff we breathe in L.A."

"Yes, Ma'am." He gave her the thumbs up sign.

They both stopped and inhaled a hearty dose of diesel exhaust. Choking, sputtering, and laughing, Thai said, "This, Miss McCoy, is the last time I take your advice about anything."

"Sorry, I forgot about the bus. Wait until you get a whiff of the pine scent, guaranteed exhaust free. You'll think you've died and gone to heaven. But look around. Have you ever seen such a great place?" This was her third staff trip up here and her love for the camp and the mountains grew each time.

"I've got to admit, you're right. Lots of trees, lots of mountains in the backdrop, and lots of sunshine. I'd forgotten how blue the sky really is. After three months in L.A., I thought it had permanently turned gray."

Kinsy chuckled. "Some places in the world, blue is still the color." She looked up to prove her point and shivered against the slight breeze.

"Over here for cabin assignments," James, the administration minister called out. "Lunch is ready now in the dining hall. Then you'll have an hour to get your things, unpack, and settle in. We'll meet back here at three. Come in grubby clothes, preferably long pants and long sleeves."

"I'll meet you for lunch in a few minutes. See the large wood-sided building?" Kinsy pointed off to her left. "That's the place."

"Meet you there," Thai agreed.

Kinsy searched for her bags. After digging through a pile, she unearthed her things. Then she got her room assignment. Since there were fewer women on staff than men, the men got the larger dorms up the hill and to the right.

Kinsy and the other seven women were assigned the house and a trailer off to the left, just beyond the dining hall, hidden in a clump of trees. She headed for the trailer and plopped her stuff on a top bunk in the back bedroom. After a quick lunch with her team, she unpacked.

Then she found a quiet spot on a log to sit and contemplate life. Well, at least to contemplate Thai. His eyes verified that he was aware of the undercurrents between them. With each minute she spent in his company, she liked him more. Wonder how I'd look as a bleached blond? She'd experienced prejudice many times, but never expected bias from another Vietnamese person. If only he'd let God heal his past, maybe—just maybe—they'd have a future.

At three, she found the guys from her team. Her dad passed out colored scarves; theirs were red. "Tie those around your necks," he instructed. James started passing out paint ball guns, goggles with nose- and mouth-guards attached, and paint balls. Each team got little marble-sized paint balls to match their scarves. About half of them fit in Kinsy's gun canister, the rest she shoved into the various pockets of her overalls.

He explained the rules of the game and the boundaries. The object was to splatter as many people as possible with red paint while not taking a hit. Points were given for the number of hits, and bonus points went to the team with the least paint splatters on them.

Kinsy and her team huddled together, discussing strategy.

"Let's stay close together, watch each other's backs," Rob whispered. He grabbed her hand. "Kinsy and I will partner. You guys keep us in sight." He led her off through the tall pines toward the playing field.

Kinsy glanced back at Thai who scowled at Rob. A warm glow spread through Kinsy. She hoped he was jealous.

"Are you dating Thai?" Rob asked when Chris and Thai were out of sight.

"No. What prompted you to ask?"

"The vibes. The way you two gaze at each other. The way he looked just now when I took your hand."

"You're imagining things. We barely know each other." Yet it seemed like she knew him better than others, like Rob, whom she'd known much longer.

"But you'd like to," Rob suggested. His hazel eyes dared her to deny his claim.

"I never said that."

"You didn't have to. Hey, how come we've never gone out?"

"Oh, Rob, you know you're like a brother to me."

"No, I can't take it!" He covered his ears with his hands. "Not the dreaded B-word, every guy's worst nightmare."

He pulled her behind a tree, giving her the quiet sign. They got their guns in position and fired on the enemy. Splat, splat, splat, splat. The orange team now had a few red blotches. Kinsy and Rob ran through the forest, dodging low tree limbs, before the orange team retaliated.

Thai and Chris caught up with them. They'd gotten the same three guys from the other side. They were whispering and laughing. Splat, splat, splat. Blue paint splotched their legs. Chris shot a couple of them in the rear as they retreated.

"Follow us," Thai said. He and Chris led out this time. A twig snapped behind her. She spun around and raised her gun. She got a green ball in the belly, and hit a tree with her return shot.

"Ouch, these things sting, Rob," she whispered.

He motioned her to follow. They came up on Chris and Thai being bombarded from several directions with several colors. They ducked and ran since they were out-numbered about two to ten.

Kinsy and Rob took cover and opened fire on the other teams. They both got several good shots. She'd completely lost track of Chris and Thai. There was no way to find them without trekking through heavily dominated enemy territory, so they went back the way they came.

"Do you get the feeling they're ganging up on us?" Kinsy whispered. "They didn't shoot at each other, but they all shot at us."

"You noticed too?" Thai asked from behind them. "Am I

being dragged into some vendetta from a previous year?"

"I'll bet the staff is getting you two goons back for all the practical jokes and Super Soaker episodes." Kinsy pointed to Rob and Chris.

"I think Kinsy and I will follow you two for awhile," Thai informed them. "I'm not interested in paying your debts, Rob. Lead on."

Rob looked at Kinsy. "Sorry, but Thai's right," she said. "This war has nothing to do with us. We'll be a few paces behind, help when we can, but we're not taking the brunt of this. You're on your own."

Chris and Rob started out. Kinsy looked at Thai and laughed out loud. "You look like a Christmas tree with a variety of different colored bulbs hanging all over you."

He yanked her downward, and she fell in a heap beside him. The ground's dampness seeped through her overalls while the smell of wet grass filled each breath. Several paint balls whizzed over them, hitting a tree. "Those were meant for us," he whispered.

His gaze fixed on hers and neither moved. Whether a second or several minutes passed, she had no idea. His smoldering eyes sent her heart pounding, and her mouth went dry. He hesitantly touched her face, running the tips of his fingers over her high cheekbone. His tenderness sent an ache through her, an ache for him to care about her the same way she'd begun caring for him.

He plucked a twig from her hair and tossed it aside. Entwining his fingers in her hair, he began closing the inches separating them. With every fiber of her being, she longed for his kiss, but at what cost? So she could cry herself to sleep every night when he replaced her with his American dream?

Kinsy forced herself to break the spell he'd unknowingly

cast over them. She rose up on an elbow and aimed for a lightness she was miles from capturing. "The gallant knight routine again, huh?"

"Yes." He brushed the dirt of her cheek. "My poor, distressed damsel."

She replayed his words. *My poor distressed damsel.* He'd said *my* not *the* or *a*, but he called her his. *I'm overreacting and having a bout of wishful dreaming.*

❧

Rising slowly and searching the horizon for other teams, Thai spotted no one. He reached down, took Kinsy's hand, and helped her up. Her hand rested snug and safe in his, and he realized he liked touching her. He'd almost kissed her! Where did his brain go when she was around? He released her hand and immediately missed the warmth. They quietly made their way down the hill, in the direction Rob and Chris had headed.

Thai grabbed Kinsy and pulled her behind a tree. He raised his gun. Splat, he got an orange guy's arm. Another splat. Kinsy got him, too, in the leg. They crept on through the dense forest. "Watch your footing," he whispered when he slid a couple of feet down the hill, causing a few rocks to roll down ahead of them.

Suddenly, they were being hit from all sides. He tried to shield and protect her. They ran as fast as they could, but hit after hit slammed against their backs with a rhythm that mimicked a machine gun's staccato release.

❧

Mama took the boys for a morning walk down river. They laughed, skipped, and sang songs. But unexpected explosions dashed aside their revelry and riveted their attention on the village. Smoke billowed across the sun-filled sky. Grabbing their hands, Mama ran fast—faster than Thai's legs would go—away from their little fishing village.

Thai fell, hitting the unyielding earth with a thud. He screamed out in pain. Mama yelled at him to hush, and her horror-filled eyes scared him into silence. She swept him up into her arms, grabbed Loi's hand, and kept running. He looked back over her shoulder as the remains of their village collapsed wall by wall, while fire destroyed building after building.

Mama fell to her knees, too tired to run any farther. Lying in the tall grass, they remained hidden until sunset. Mama's quiet weeping wounded Thai more than seeing the burning village. The rest of their family was most likely dead. Thai cried until he fell asleep. When he awoke, near-darkness surrounded them and his stomach gnawed with hunger. An eerie silence penetrated his spirit, leaving him empty and cold.

❧

The whistle blew, signifying the end of the war. Relief flooded Thai as he stopped running. An exhausted Kinsy, her breathing heavy, leaned against him. She stumbled to the nearest log where she plopped down. "Now I understand being saved by the bell!" Scrutinizing him, she asked, "You okay?"

"Fine," he barked. The memory that shook him to the core made his words more brusque than he intended. Kinsy's imploring gaze made him force a smile he was far from feeling. "Let's find Chris and Rob," he said more gently. When they did, all four of them resembled clowns in polka dotted attire. Laughing, they all shared their tales of war. Thai joined them, but his laughter rang hollow.

"They hurt worse when they bounce off and don't break open. Look at this welt," Kinsy said, rolling up the right sleeve of her navy blue turtleneck.

"Oh, poor baby," Rob said with no sympathy.

When the scores were tallied, the red team came in dead last. They all protested they'd been ganged up on. No one had much sympathy because at one time or another, they'd all been the butt of a Rob-and-Chris style joke.

"I'm hitting the shower fellows. I'll see you at dinner," Kinsy informed her team. "Hopefully without green hair."

"I'll walk you back," Rob offered.

Thai watched Kinsy walk away with Rob. An uneasiness settled in his gut. He tried not to notice them as they laughed and joked together, but his attention kept wandering in their direction. At her door, Kinsy raised up on tiptoe and kissed Rob's cheek. Envy—an emotion he was unaccustomed to before meeting Kinsy—shot through his veins. *Why should I waste time on jealousy? She's a long way from the blue-eyed blond you're waiting for, pal.*

After a long, hot shower, Thai met his team for dinner. Kinsy, her usual eager, energetic self, didn't give Rob any more attention than she gave him or Chris. Thai almost asked her about her relationship with Rob, but figured the same question twice in one day was too much. Being male, he sensed Rob's interest, and the kiss on Rob's cheek made him wonder about Kinsy.

After dinner, they met up at Star Rock for a praise service. For the next hour, they did nothing but sing praise songs to the Lord. Then each team went off to pray for their ministries. By the time they'd finished, Thai decided he was crazy to care what happened between Kinsy and Rob. Thai certainly wasn't interested in her. Not in the least.

Then why did I almost kiss her? The moment just caught him off guard. Nothing more than being close to a beautiful woman whose lips begged him to taste their sweetness, touch their softness. *Yeah, and pigs fly.* His attraction for

Kinsy went way beyond her lips. The woman exemplified everything he'd dreamed of. *Except the added bonus of her Asian heritage,* he thought bitterly.

They spent the next morning playing wild and crazy team games. The red team fared much better, though they still didn't win. In the dining hall after lunch, Karl announced each team had free time until chapel at seven. He gave them a list of some ways to spend the afternoon and several options for dinner.

"Golf!" Chris said with excitement.

"Definitely," Rob agreed.

"No question. Who would fish when they could golf?" Thai asked.

"Me," Kinsy threw out weakly.

"You? What are you thinking, woman?" Rob asked.

"I don't know how to golf." Kinsy looked at each of them suspiciously. Eyes squinted, she asked, "Did you guys bring your clubs?"

All three nodded.

"You conspired behind my back?" She stood placing hands on her hips.

"No," Thai assured her. "Rob sent Chris and me an E-mail suggesting we drag our clubs along, you know—just in case."

"How come Rob didn't include me in the E-mail since I'm part of this team?" She raised her eyebrows.

Rob had the decency to blush. "I knew you weren't a golfer."

"And yet you expect me to spend my afternoon with you on a golf course?" she challenged.

Thai knew Kinsy was only giving Rob a hard time, but Rob chewed his lip in uncertainty. "She's got you there, pal." Thai said.

Rob held up his hands. "Now wait a minute, three of us voted for golf and majority rules. We've already made a deal, whoever wins the first hole will be your personal tutor."

"Fine. I'll be a good sport, even though this whole thing seems underhanded to me. But if there are any more choices, I'd better be included from the onset." She emphasized her point by waving her index finger under Rob's nose.

"Yes, Ma'am." Rob saluted.

Thai loved golf. Him, God, and a ball out in the wide-open spaces—not much in life better than that. Especially on a beautiful course with the backdrop of the Sierra Nevadas surrounding him.

He pulled his club from his bag, lined up his first shot, and swung. The ball soared toward the hole, landing neatly on the green, just feet from the desired destination. With a mixture of dread and anticipation, he was certain Kinsy was his for the afternoon. He exchanged his nine iron for his putter and sank the birdie.

Chris managed to par, and Rob bogied. "You can have the girl." Rob did a gangster impression. "She's yours, pal. You teach her to play—if you can. Meanwhile Chris and I will see you two later." They hopped in their golf cart and headed over the hill.

"What are par, bogie, and birdie?" A light breeze played with her hair, and Thai remembered its silky softness from yesterday.

He pulled out a wood for Kinsy to try. "Par is when you break even. This hole, a par three, meaning a golfer should get the ball into the hole in three shots. Chris managed that, so he got par. A bogie is one shot over par, and a birdie is one shot under par."

"Seems to me the worst guy should have gotten stuck with me."

Thai tensed at her statement. "Would you rather golf with Rob? I could finagle a trade." He hoped his disappointment didn't seep out with his words.

"Not necessarily. I just thought you might enjoy the game more if you weren't saddled with me."

Thai decided now looked like a good time to test the water. He casually leaned on his club. "You know, I think Rob might like to meet a damsel in distress, especially if she were you."

"Oh and what makes you think so?" She cocked her head to the right, raising her eyebrows.

"Guys know these things."

"Oh, they do, huh? Well then you also know I'm not interested in Rob, and he's not interested in me either. He's just lonely and between dates. He's another guy who goes for blonds." Her pointed look chided him for his narrow thinking. "I may have to become acquainted with Preference. I'm sure I'm worth it. Now teach me to hit this silly ball."

"Blonds, huh?" he asked, handing her his wood.

She took the club, and he placed a ball on the tee for her. "Those are the kinds of girls he dates. Blonds. Airheaded, breathy types." She lined up her shot and actually looked like she knew what she was doing until she swung. She clipped the top of the ball, and the thing barely moved. However, her club flew several yards into the air and landed with a thud against the emerald-colored grass.

"The goal is for the ball to fly out there and the club to stay in your hand." He grinned at her and realized he no longer thought of his mother and the explosion every single time he glanced at Kinsy. As a matter of fact, on this trip the memories had only plagued him during that paintball game. The rest of the time, his mind had been preoccupied with a sassy gal who claimed she might try Preference. But Thai didn't think blond suited her—not in the least.

She rolled her eyes and retrieved her club. "I thought you were my teacher." She handed him the club. "So teach me."

Another group of golfers drove up. "We'll let them go first." He and Kinsy moved out of the way. "Do you know any nice girls for Rob? Non-bimbo types?"

Kinsy thought a minute. "My roommate, Danielle, would be perfect. Unfortunately, she also has the wrong hair color."

He ignored her jab. "Maybe we can do something as a foursome sometime. See if your prediction proves correct." He wondered if he were using Rob as an excuse to spend more time with Kinsy.

"Maybe," she said, distracted as she studied each golfer teeing off. When they finished and drove their cart on, Kinsy moved back to the tee. She stretched her neck muscles by tilting her head from side to side. "I'm ready. What are the basics?"

Thai stepped up next to her. "Eye on the ball."

"Check."

"Feet shoulder-width apart."

She adjusted her stance. "Check."

"Knees bent."

First-time golfers usually looked corny, so Thai tried not to laugh.

"What now?"

"Swing easy. Don't try to kill the ball."

She swung, made contact, the ball sliced to the right and only rolled about twenty-five yards.

"Much better!" Thai hoped to encourage her.

"Don't lie to me!" Her face set, she marched out to reclaim her ball. "I'd say that was a pathetic improvement at best."

She sat the ball on the tee and tried again. The results were much the same. After three more tries, Thai offered to help at a closer range. He'd hoped to avoid this scenario, but Kinsy's mounting frustration made eluding physical contact impossible.

Thai stood behind her and wrapped his arms around hers, gripping the club with her. Her hair smelled like apple blossoms, and a silky strand of her short locks blew against his cheek. A flash of his mother's hair tickling his cheek was blotted out by the memory of yesterday's near-kiss. As Thai had imagined, Kinsy fit perfectly in his arms, and concentrating on his swing challenged him to the max.

"Eye on the ball, feet apart, knees slightly bent, now we'll swing easy. Relax, let me lead." He led her through the swing. They connected with the ball and followed the shot through. Neither of them moved. The ball went much farther and higher than Kinsy's previous shots and almost hit the green.

"Did you feel the poetry in motion as you followed through on your swing?"

Kinsy nodded. Thai slowly loosened his hold and moved away from her. His true desire was to turn her in his arms, look into those almond eyes, and see if he affected her the way she did him. Did she experience all the crazy things he did? Did her heart beat like a tom-tom when he held her? Did she almost forget to breathe?

"Now what?" Kinsy asked softly, seeming a bit unnerved.

"Now you take your second shot." He threw his golf

bag over his right shoulder.

"I think I'll try this one by myself." She began walking the distance toward her ball.

Good idea. Thai glanced toward the golf cart but decided to follow Kinsy on foot. The walk would help him work off some of the tension from that close encounter.

When they arrived at the ball, he handed her the correct club. She lined herself up with the hole. "Eye on the ball, feet apart, knees bent, swing easy," she reminded herself. After four more tries, her ball rolled into the hole. Thai admired her tenacity.

"Double bogie. Not bad for your first-ever hole of golf."

She smiled up and him. "Shall we move on?"

"We shall."

They walked backed to the golf cart. Thai had some thinking to do. Kinsy wasn't anywhere close to the woman of his dreams, or at least the one he thought he dreamed of. Yet he could no longer deny his growing emotions. Everything about her captivated him. Everything except her Vietnamese heritage. *But is that even important anymore?* Memories of that exploding village rushed upon him. His mother's gentle weeping swept over his mind as if she were with him. Thai cringed, and forced himself not to bolt from all that Kinsy represented.

❧

Kinsy lined up her next shot. *Did you feel the poetry in motion?* Thai's question echoed through her mind. *Yeah, but the poetry she encountered when he wrapped his arms around her had nothing to do with her swing. The question was, did she affect him at all?*

Other than occasional small talk, they finished their next few holes in quiet contemplation. They hadn't even started the fifth hole when Rob and Chris showed up.

They'd already finished their entire game on the nine-hole course.

Thai and Kinsy decided to quit. Rob told Kinsy she could pick their dinner spot since she'd been a good sport about golf. She chose Ducey's. They drove to The Pines Resort where the restaurant sat overlooking Bass Lake. Requesting an outdoor table, they admired the evening sun, ducking behind the mountains and tall pines. The serenity calmed Kinsy's jumbled emotions.

After they'd ordered, they sat quietly while the waves lapped upon the shore. Taking a deep breath of the crisp mountain air, Kinsy admired God's handprint on the sky; He'd brushed hues of orange, pink, and lavender across the western expanse.

Soon the waitress returned with their iced teas, and Chris ended their contemplative moment. "I hate to break the silence, but Karl asked us to share with each other the best part of our jobs on staff at CC," he said, stirring a packet of sugar into his tea.

"For me," Kinsy said, gaze never leaving the sunset. "Getting to travel to places I've never been and tell people who've never heard the good news about Christ." She smiled. "God gave me the perfect job because traveling and evangelism are my passions." She squeezed her lemon into her tea glass.

"College kids are at the brink of many major decisions," Thai said. "If I can encourage one of them to make a better choice about dating, friendships, or their futures, it makes my week. Every choice we make either moves us toward God or away from Him. My goals are to help them understand that concept and to equip them through the study of God's Word to make decisions and strengthen their tie to Christ."

Kinsy and Thai exchanged a glance of mutual respect. He no longer shied away from looking at her, and the pain crossed his face less frequently. Her chest tightened. She refocused her gaze on the lake. Kinsy yearned for him to fall for her as she was falling for him. Yet maybe for Thai this was all part of his brother's experiment. Her stomach clenched.

"Rob, what's your favorite part of working at CC?" Chris asked.

"Eating peanut butter from my armpit."

"Gross!" Kinsy scrunched up her nose.

"The junior highers love gross. Seriously, watching God change the heart of a rebellious middle-schooler tops anything. Many of them come into my department with an adolescent attitude, and they leave two years later desiring to live their lives for God."

They all looked at Chris. "Baptizing a new believer. I can't ever immerse someone without getting teary. Here is a high schooler willing to publicly proclaim to the world he's chosen to follow Christ and now is moving forward into a new life. Chokes me up every time."

While the waitress passed out the plates, Kinsy thought about how extraordinary each of these men was. They'd committed their lives to shepherding God's flock, and they loved what they did. Their faces reflected their joy. Even though each of them was special to her, only Thai pulled her heartstrings.

She took a bite of her salad. "Chris, how are Miranda and the baby?"

"They are great. My favorite thing in life is spending time with my wife and baby daughter."

"You're married?" Thai asked. "I had no idea."

"Five years next month. I highly recommend tying the

knot." He grinned at Thai and winked.

Kinsy cleared her throat. So both Chris and Rob had noticed the sparks between her and Thai.

"So how'd your golf game end up today?" Thai asked.

The three of them spent the rest of dinner talking golf. Relieved that she didn't have to carry on witty conversation, Kinsy ate in silence, watching the sun sink out of sight. Her emotions were on overload and she relished the time to think things through. Did Thai even have a clue about the way he affected her? Probably not. Kinsy's heart sank right along with the sun.

When they got back to camp, they headed up the trail toward Star Rock. Tonight her dad taught on the ministry gifts and how God used them all in His body, the church. Kinsy thought about the three guys on her team, how different they each were, yet how perfectly suited they were for their ministries.

Tired, Kinsy bid her teammates good night as soon as chapel ended. Thai offered to walk her up the trail, but she declined. Her ravaged emotions couldn't take being around him for another minute.

Oh, God, what am I going to do? I like him way too much, but I'm the wrong nationality and have the wrong hair color.

Deep within her heart, Kinsy was reminded that God knew the plans He had for her. She'd hang on to Him.

five

Thai rose before dawn the next morning, needing some solid God-time before he faced Kinsy and Half Dome. He slipped out of the cabin, leaving behind a symphony of seven snoring men. He spent the next hour sitting on a tree stump, praying and studying the Word. He told God all about his confusion regarding Kinsy. No answers came, but the time with his Father refreshed him.

At five-thirty, they all boarded the bus and headed toward the drop-off point that would begin the hike of a lifetime. During this journey, his team sat in the very front and were the first to enjoy the breathtaking view. Kinsy took the seat next to Chris, so Thai claimed the window seat across the aisle. He enjoyed the ride, drinking in all the sights along the way.

They passed through Wawona Tunnel and into Yosemite Valley. On the left was El Capitan and then Yosemite falls. Walls of sculpted granite intensified the majesty of God's creation. Off to the right, Thai spotted Sentinel Dome. Kinsy's describing Yosemite as awesome seemed almost inadequate.

The bus stopped near Curry Village. Thai grabbed his backpack. Chris and Kinsy waited for him and Rob, and they exited together.

"What do you think?" she asked.

He shook his head. "I can't find the words."

She nodded her agreement.

"Shall we start our ascent?" Chris asked. "Sad thing is we start by going down, then we have a longer uphill trek." He led out with Rob on his heels.

"After you, Kinsy." He planned to watch out for her, in case she got into trouble.

"I'm not fond of heights. I may slow you down."

"I don't mind." Even more reason for him to keep an eye on her. Thai followed her down the narrow dirt trail, eyeing Half Dome in the distance. "Hard to believe we'll be on top of that rock in a few hours."

"My mind is saying, 'yeah, right, seems impossible.' It looks so high and so far away."

"Hey, where's the Kinsy I know? The one who rises to every challenge?"

"I think I left her back at camp," she joked. "What if I can't, Thai? What if I'm too out of shape? I'm so inadequate. Look at that mountain of granite. Who am I to think I can conquer the magnificent Half Dome?"

"You can, Kinsy. You're in great shape." He believed every word he said. He'd never met a more capable person. "Don't you accomplish everything you set out to do?"

"Usually."

"Remember you and the golf ball yesterday? This is just another challenge set before you. Think of the excitement cresting the last ridge. We'll be on top of the world."

"You're right. I know you are." The words belied her lack of conviction.

Thai almost chuckled at the irony of his words. Kinsy struggled with the physical aspects of the climb, but he struggled spiritually with his ascent toward Christlikeness. Inadequacy seeped from his pores. In all honesty, he didn't trust God with his past, or his future. That's why he'd figured everything out for himself, down to the type of person he'd even consider dating. Kinsy didn't fit his ideal, but did she fit God's?

"I'm anxious to have this climb behind me." She grinned back at him. "I won't think about the distance. I can do everything through Him who gives me strength, even this."

"That's my girl."

Kinsy glanced back again, a question on her face, and he realized his faux pas. A part of him yearned for nothing more than for Kinsy McCoy to be his girl. An energetic little dynamo, she'd blown into his life like a fresh breeze and turned his world topsy-turvy. All the things he was sure of now seemed questionable.

Thai had decided years ago he'd only date the all American girl—blond and blue eyed, so he'd have a chance at American normalcy. A chance to forget his painful past, maybe even forget he came from Vietnam.

A great plan he'd stuck to since age twelve. He'd never even dated a brunette. Then this little fresh-faced Vietnamese beauty with a heart bigger than she was, caused him to doubt his decisions. Thai prided himself in being a striver. He fixed his eye on the goal and never veered. How did one tiny woman manage to push him so far off course?

Kinsy stopped and leaned against a boulder. Rob and Chris had disappeared, hidden from their view by the surrounding forest. A bunny hopped across the path, and chirping birds serenaded them with their song of spring. Kinsy took a few sips of water, rubbed her right calf, and they continued.

By the time they reached Heartbreak Hill, the trees had become sparse and rocks lay everywhere. She smiled weakly and looked at the trail ahead. He followed close behind as she began the extreme uphill trek. About halfway up, Thai realized this hill was appropriately named. His heart broke watching Kinsy fight her way to the top. They climbed for what seemed like forever, dirt crunching under their feet with each step. This was definitely the most intense part of the journey so far.

Thai wasn't sure exactly how long this portion took, but he was certain they'd climbed at least two hours, going straight up toward the sun. His legs wobbled, and he wondered if they'd carry him the rest of the way. Kinsy must wonder, too. Her steps had slowed to a snail's pace.

When they crested Heartbreak Hill, Thai said, "We're almost there."

Kinsy stopped. He put an arm around her, and she leaned against him. She laid her head against his chest and closed her eyes.

"You're doing great," he crooned.

"My legs feel like rubber."

"Mine, too."

She took a deep breath. "Let's go."

He gave her a squeeze and released his hold. They went down for a short way—a welcome change to his aching calves. Then the trail headed up again. Finally, they reached The One Thousand Steps. Rocks in the mountain created steps leading to the base of Half Dome.

"Do you really think there are actually one thousand of them?"

Thai shrugged. "I have no idea."

Kinsy led out again. When they reached the base, she said, "There were at least a thousand, if not two."

Thai chuckled in appreciation of her attempt at humor.

❧

Kinsy studied the two, thick wire cables, running from the

base to the top of Half Dome. Fear knotted her stomach. Terrified of heights, how could she do this?

Thai wrapped her in another hug. He must have read the terror she knew was written across her face. "I'll be right behind you," he promised.

She nodded. Inside she longed to head down the mountain as fast as she could run. Instead, she grabbed a pair of gardening gloves from the huge pile on the ground near the cables, and slipped them on.

"Pull yourself up the face of the rock using your arms and the cables," Thai stated the obvious.

Kinsy bit her lip and grasped the cables. She tugged herself slowly higher, placing her feet wherever they'd plant. *God, please don't let me lose my grip. And don't let me think about falling.*

Two climbers were coming down using the same two cables.

"Thai?" Her raspy voice echoed her fear.

"Don't worry. Just move to the right and let them pass."

She nodded and followed his instructions, heaving a big sigh once the other hikers passed her.

"I'm right behind you. You're doing great. Not too much farther. Keep moving up."

She nodded, searching for another solid place to stick her foot. A loose pebble caused her foot to slip slightly, and she nearly screamed.

"Good job, Kins. Keep going, baby. Keep going."

His endearment touched her heart. She had to make the top, just so she could fall into his arms.

"The view is beautiful from up here. Can you believe how far we can see?"

"I'm not looking. I'm only staring at my shoes."

"Just keep looking at those shoes. You're doing great. I'm so proud of you."

Finally, the top. Every muscle in Kinsy entire body ached and her arms throbbed. "Thank you, Lord. Thank you," she wept softly.

Thai held her. "Now you can look. Breathtaking is the only word for this." He waved his arm as if he owned the grand expanse before them.

Breathtaking was right. An eagle soared overhead. The air seemed lighter and thinner, the clouds much closer. Looking over the vista, toward the peaks and valleys, Kinsy recognized God's signature in every direction. The Creator of the universe must have smiled when He carved out Yosemite.

"Thank you, Thai," she whispered. "I couldn't have made it without you. I'd have missed all this." As she glanced at him, she saw the tenderness radiating from his eyes. "Once again, you're my gallant knight."

He brushed away her tears with his thumb. "And once again you're my beautiful distressed damsel. Rescuing you is becoming a habit." His gaze intensified. "A habit I'm not sure I plan to break."

Kinsy thought he might kiss her, but Rob cleared his throat, reminding them they had an audience. Thai kept his arm around her, and together they admired the view.

"It's incredible," Kinsy whispered. Then her gusto returned. "We're on top of Half Dome! What a sense of accomplishment!"

Thai beamed at her.

"I can see forever! Is the view amazing or what?" She held tightly to him and turned carefully, looking out in all directions. The loose gravel under her feet made her think slipping off the edge wouldn't be too difficult, so she used Thai as her anchor.

"You're what's amazing," he whispered near her ear. Goosebumps covered her arms.

"I'm Amerasian," she solemnly reminded him.

"I know, but that doesn't seem to matter. . .much."

"But it still matters?"

"I don't know. All I know is you're terrific."

She smiled. "So are you, Thai."

"I want to kiss you right now," he said, caressing her face. "But I won't. Our first kiss should be a sacred moment—just between us."

His words touched her heart. His eyes promised that, in not too much longer, she'd know the tenderness of his lips against hers.

"Over here for a team shot," Rob motioned.

Kinsy clung to Thai. They inched their way toward Chris and Rob. "Go slowly," she whispered. "I feel like we're going to slip off the edge."

"What would you do if you didn't have him to hold on to?" Rob asked.

"I'd crawl." And she had no doubt she would. They all laughed at her honesty.

Other teams were arriving now. Some of them had a member or two quit and turn back. Kinsy had no doubt she would have been one of them if it had not been for Thai.

She looked up at him and knew the possibility existed to love this man. *God, please don't let him break my heart. Somehow, let him love me, too.*

After half an hour and many pictures, the time to leave arrived. Kinsy couldn't wait to have her feet on flat ground. Though the scenery was beautiful, she was ready to head back down. Thai stayed by her side, keeping her safe. Her dad gave her a knowing wink, and Kinsy smiled at him.

Both she and Thai put their gloves back on for the climb down the cables. "Going down won't be as bad," he assured her. "I'll go first."

He started down the rock the most common way—face forward. A couple of guys just ahead of them even ran down the cables. Kinsy's head spun just watching them. She opted to back down, facing the rock. Going forward and seeing everything, including the heights to which they'd climbed, was just too much. Again, she kept her eyes fixed on her feet. Thai coached her down, telling her where to place each step.

He said going down would be easier. Boy, was he wrong! Even after she finished with the cables, the trek remained difficult. Bone tired, she didn't voice her discouragement. At least going up, there was a goal, the prize of accomplishment waiting to greet her at the top of Half Dome. Her knees ached from the constant downward motion. Weary, she longed to see the end of the trail. When they finally arrived at the bus several hours later, Thai hugged her and kissed her temple.

"I'm so proud of you! Look at all the men from CC who quit, but you didn't give in to your fears."

She smiled. "Definitely a hard day, but a great one." *Mostly great because of you.* "I'm glad we're back on semi-flat ground. Thank you for not letting me quit."

Thai pulled her behind a massive oak. He touched her hair and her face, gently tracing her jaw line. She couldn't believe this was happening. "You are my inspiration."

"For what?" Her voice quivered.

"Kinsy, I've spent my life running from my past, and I'm getting tired of running. I don't want to give in to my fears anymore. I'm beginning to think I'm ready to take a chance on you—on us. I'm not going to say I'm free of everything that happened to me, but I do think I'm starting to grow. . .at least, some. Is there any way you would be interested in—"

"I am. I have been since our game of basketball."

He lowered his head. Their lips met. For Kinsy, Thai's kiss was the fourth of July and Christmas rolled into one. When the kiss ended, his expression matched the emotions dancing in her heart.

He drew her to him and held her close. Neither spoke. Words proved unnecessary. None were capable of describing all the sensations manifesting themselves within her. But thanks to God poured from her heart. He'd heard and answered her prayers: Thai saw past her Asian features to the woman inside.

six

Thai whistled on the drive to work the following Monday morning. Spring was here. Flowers bloomed, birds sang, and he just might be in "serious like." The silly ear-to-ear grin plastered across his face witnessed his delightful dilemma. Since last Wednesday afternoon when he'd kissed Kinsy, the grin had become an almost permanent part of him. If not for the occasional nightmares that were a regular part of his sleep pattern, Thai wondered if the smile would have remained intact even when he slept.

With his usual precision, Thai buried the pain and chose to focus on Kinsy. Ah, Kinsy. Man was she terrific. They hadn't kissed again—yet. He planned to be careful, go slow, set good boundaries. They also avoided public displays of affection; PDA as the college kids called it. But just the secret looks and her just-for-him smile curled his toes.

Last night after church, they strolled along Kinsy's favorite stretch of beach. Hand in hand, they walked for a couple of hours. Neither said much. They didn't have to. Being together was enough.

Thai parked next to her car. Even seeing the Del Sol brought him pleasure. He decided to drop by her office before heading to his. He'd start his day with a ray of her smile to carry him through.

"Good morning, Miss McCoy," he said as he rounded the corner into her office.

She looked up from the papers on her desk. No smile

greeted him from her pale face. He knew immediately something was wrong—very wrong.

"Kinsy?"

"Thai, I'm glad you're here." She rose from her desk. "We need to talk. Please, have a seat." She motioned to the padded chairs facing her desk, her words stiff and formal. Walking around him, she shut her office door. Her blue plaid jumper swished around her ankles with an ominous finality.

Kinsy's face was drawn and tight. Even her movements seemed wooden and unnatural. She returned to the chair behind her desk, keeping distance between them.

"What's going on?" He tugged at the collar of his denim shirt, suddenly choking him, even though the first button was open.

"I talked to Steve this morning." She took a deep breath. "Our Bible smuggling trip is set. We're going to Vietnam."

He felt like she'd stabbed him in the back. The explosion flashed in his mind. He pictured Loi's and his mother's bloodied, stiff bodies in a heap of smoke and ash. Thai's heart pounded, and every breath hurt.

The present swam before his eyes, and anger flooded him. He rose, leaning over Kinsy's desk, hitting it with a clenched fist. "You did this on purpose!"

"N–no, Thai, not on purpose. Steve was ultimately responsible for our destination. I just—"

"You just cooperated!"

Kinsy reached for him, but he instinctively jerked back before she made contact. She looked down. The pain on her face in no way compared to the hurt and betrayal slicing his heart to shreds.

"I told you the day we met I would never return—not ever!" He leaned farther across her desk and got in her face. "Just because you have some fantasy about returning to your homeland, don't drag me into your plans. Vietnam was a nightmare I don't plan to relive."

"Thai, I'm sorry." A tear crept down her cheek. Her eyes begged for understanding, but Thai was incapable of anything but personal agony. Her shoulders sagged with the weight of a bad decision.

"Why?," he asked in a pain-filled voice. "Why did you do this to me?"

"I told you I wasn't responsible for the final decision, except prayer. You'll have to take this up with God." A defensive edge hardened her words.

He ran a hand through his hair and paced her small office like a caged animal. Finally, he returned to the chair.

Looking her square in the eye, he said, "I can't—I won't go back. Even if it costs me my job. If need be, I'll turn in my resignation today."

"No, Thai. Please don't. We'll try to work around this somehow."

"Kinsy, you don't seem to understand. There is no working around it. I will not—I repeat—will not ever set foot on Vietnamese soil as long as I live!" With his vehement declaration, Thai left Kinsy's office, closing the door more forcefully than he'd intended.

He headed down the hall to his office corridor. His conscience pricked. *What if God asked me to go? Would I tell Him no? Surely, He wouldn't ask that from me.*

Thai spent the morning arguing with himself and struggling with guilt over his reaction. Why did he assume the worst? Maybe she really had nothing to do with it all. He'd never known her to lie. He picked up the phone and dialed her extension.

Kinsy's voice greeted him. "I'll be out of the office Monday afternoon. You may either leave a message or press 135 to speak to my secretary."

He pressed 135. "Judy, where's Kinsy?"

"She decided to take a personal day about ten this morning. Did you keep her out too late last night? She didn't look well."

"How did you know I was with Kinsy last night?"

"You two are the talk of the office. Did you think you could date the pastor's daughter and no one would notice?'

"I suppose not." He sighed and hung up his phone.

Great. The entire office probably also knew they'd had a fight. Their first. He decided to go buy an I'm-sorry-I-was-a-jerk card and leave it on her desk. Nothing had changed. He wouldn't be a party to the trip, but he shouldn't have blamed Kinsy. He'd practically called her a liar. After purchasing the perfect card with a pathetic looking dog on the front, he returned to the office, sat at her desk, and scrawled a short note.

Kinsy, I'm sorry. I overreacted. I know this isn't your fault. Forgive me for insinuating it was. Though I won't go on the trip, I hope we can still be us. Fondly, Thai.

Some of the heaviness lifted. He sealed the envelope and leaned it against Kinsy's phone. Picking up a framed picture of her and her six sisters caused his heart to warm. He replaced the frame and rose to leave. A letter on the corner of her desk caught his eye. The letterhead indicated it was about the Bible smuggling trip.

Thai hesitated. Since he was supposed to be a co-leader on the trip, reading the contents probably wouldn't hurt. He picked up the letter, his hand shaking slightly. Guilt pricked his conscience, but he read on. The last paragraph caused him to sit back down. He read it again.

I so appreciate your openness and even your suggestion that the CC team take the humanitarian aid trip to Vietnam. Your excitement about the possibility of visiting Vietnam when we spoke on the phone two weeks ago confirmed what I already suspected. I am confident this is where the Lord is sending your team, so congratulations, Miss McCoy, your dreams and prayers are coming to fruition.

He stared at the letter, disappointment and hurt battling within. She'd known all along—not only known, but requested the destination. He scanned to the top of the page and read the date. April 1. Within the past couple of weeks she'd asked for Vietnam as the team's destination, knowing full well Thai's repulsion about returning. Obviously, she didn't care.

Steve may have ultimately chosen the destination, but she suggested it, and even encouraged the decision. Thai swallowed hard. Kinsy McCoy wasn't at all the woman he assumed. He shut his eyes, hoping to close out the pain as well. She was a liar and a manipulator. All his hopes for overcoming his past now mocked him. Even more important than Kinsy's participation in this farce, she was also Vietnamese. I should have never veered from my decision to marry an all-American blond. He tossed the card in the trash. *I have been a fool. An utter fool. Kinsy McCoy won't dupe me again. Not ever.*

❧

Kinsy jogged along the beach. Boy, her life had gone from perfect to disaster in four point seven seconds. She hoped the run would clear her head, rid her of a nasty headache, and let off some steam. Just last night she and Thai had strode this same beach, and today he marched out on her in a huff.

She really wasn't surprised at how the scene played out. Even though he'd learned to accept her, he withdrew whenever Vietnam was mentioned, and his eyes were by no means void of the glimmer of pain. His words before that kiss near Half Dome now plagued her. He had said he couldn't make any promises. Perhaps today ended any hopes of even the beginning of promise. She'd give him a couple of days to think, cool off, and then they'd talk. Her stomach knotted. What if he refused to talk? *Don't borrow trouble, Kinsy.*

When the possibility of this trip presented itself almost a year ago—long before she met Thai—she sensed God answering her long prayed prayer to find her birth mother's people. Disguised as a humanitarian aid trip, its true purpose lay in smuggling Bibles to the underground church. They'd stay at an orphanage run by a Christian couple and bike Bibles to nearby villages.

Kinsy hoped to trace her family history since the orphanage was the one where the McCoys had adopted her. She already knew her mother came from a small fishing village; her father was an American G.I. The entire village rejected both mother and baby.

Somewhere in the back of her mind, she believed this trip would free Thai from his past, so he could embrace the plans God had for his future. From her perspective, this looked like the perfect opportunity to make her dreams come true and help Thai at the same time. The only problem, he didn't want her help.

She probably needed to warn her dad about this. He would know what to do and he'd pray. She jogged back to her car for the forty-minute drive home. Because of the distance, she only indulged herself with a beach jog once a week. Her dream was to someday live on the beach; she loved the ocean and its powerful reminder of her Creator. He was still in control, even though her life had hit a bump in the road.

Kinsy dropped into the car seat and punched in her dad's extension on her cell phone. "Hi, Dad." She filled him in on the earlier disagreement. "What should I do?"

"Why don't you see if you can get the trip changed and keep me posted? I don't want to lose Thai over this. Maybe God still has work to do before he can face the past. He's come a long way in a little over three months. Be patient, pumpkin."

Kinsy smiled. Her dad had been saying those three words to her since before she could remember. Patience—the elusive ability to wait. "I'll try. I love you, Dad."

"Goes double for me."

Snapping her cell phone shut, she decided to head back to the office, pick up Steve's home number, and try reaching him tonight. The sooner the better. Kinsy pulled into the parking lot. No sign of Thai's Miata. He must have left for the day.

She unlocked a back door, hoping to bypass as many eyes as possible. She still wore her jogging attire—tank top and shorts—not very appropriate for the church office. Slipping into her office, unseen, she closed the door behind her. She flipped on the light. Her chair was pushed away from her desk and turned sideways. Someone had been in there. Prickles danced up her spine and the back of her neck.

Moving slowly, cautiously toward her desk, Kinsy

wished she could control her heart's increased pace. She peeked around the corner, making certain no one was hiding there. With relief, she sat down, glanced around the room, and rolled forward toward her desk. The message light flashed on her phone. She decided to ignore the voice mail until tomorrow.

Steve's letter with his home and office number lay in the middle of her desk—one corner crumpled as if someone held on too tightly. She smoothed out the crinkles, knowing she'd left the letter on the corner of her desk, unwrinkled. Some sixth sense suggested that Thai had been snooping.

Kinsy reread the incriminating evidence in her hand. If Thai read this letter, he'd never believe she hadn't finagled the destination of this trip. Her suggesting Vietnam had taken place last summer, but from the sound of the letter, it might have happened just a couple of weeks ago. However, her encouraging Steve to continue pursuit of Vietnam had occurred after she met Thai and after she knew how painful the trip would be. She had known—almost for certain—this was their destination when she was with Thai last week in Yosemite. Yet Kinsy, fearful of his disapproval, had chosen not to mention even the possibility to him. Perhaps she had been naive. Kinsy had far more to fear than merely his disapproval. Would one dream cost her another?

She stuck the letter in a file folder to take home and decided to call Steve later tonight. Maybe Thai could forgive her if she got the trip changed to somewhere else, anywhere else. Rising to leave, something purple protruding from her trash can caught her eye. Bending down, she pulled out an envelope with her name scrawled across the front in Thai's bold script. So, he had been in there.

Tearing open the flap, she removed a greeting card. The saddest looking Basset Hound she'd ever seen looked back at her. Inside the card simply said sorry. Sitting back down, she read Thai's note to her. She rested her head against the back of her chair, closing her eyes and imagining the scenario unfolding.

Thai must have regretted their tiff as much as she had, even going out of his way to buy a card and write a note. He must have come in here to leave it on her desk, the letter caught his eye, and the desire for them to still be an "us" went straight into the garbage.

❧

Thai's sparsely furnished living room seemed as empty as his heart. The lone recliner that usually brought comfort now ridiculed his single existence. Thai muted his big screen TV. Even basketball, his favorite sport, couldn't capture his attention. He grabbed his cordless, punched in his most frequently dialed number and paced restlessly.

"Hello."

"Tong, it's me."

"Thai! How was the trip to Yosemite? I've always hoped to go myself, someday."

"The trip was great. Beautiful, incredible, amazing."

"And?" Tong asked, reading the unsaid, as always.

"Kinsy and I hit it off—too good, as a matter of fact."

"What do you mean?"

"She reeled me in." He plopped into his brand new hunter green recliner.

"Reeled you in? So, you're a fish now?"

"No, a fool." He moved the handle on his chair and the footrest rose. "I should have never veered from my determination to stick with blonds. Kinsy and I can never have a relationship. There's too much in the past—and maybe even in the present."

"You and Kinsy have a relationship now?"

"We had the beginnings of one until today, but not anymore."

"So, what happened?"

"I ended the thing. She's a smooth operator, fooled me completely, but the truth shined bright and clear this morning. For one week this woman had me right where she wanted me, but never again." He picked up the remote and surfed the muted channels.

"What in the world did she do?"

"Our Bible smuggling trip is to Vietnam! Vietnam! The very place I don't want to go, and she knew it!"

Tong's silence spoke of Thai's own shock.

"But topping that, she wasn't completely honest about the whole thing. I found a letter proving her deception."

"No kidding? From what you said, she didn't impress me as the type."

"She wanted her own way—despite how I felt. She manipulated things." Thai let the footrest down and rose from his chair. "Now she expects me to go!" He started his pacing again, all the while wondering if his reaction was really an easy escape. After all, the nightmares hadn't gone away, just because he had declared himself in "serious like" with Kinsy. Despite his silly smile when he remembered that kiss, their relationship still stirred the old fear that tainted his past.

"Wow. I don't know what to say."

"Well, I know what to say! She's not forcing me to go! Period!"

"Will you be able to get out of the trip and keep your job? I mean isn't going your responsibility since the trip is for the college kids?"

"Yeah, as the College Pastor, I'm expected to participate. But I am not going. If I have to resign, I will."

"Thai, this is your dream job. Think things through."

"I have, and I'm furious with her for putting me in this spot by using blatant female manipulation. She knows how I feel about Vietnam. Look how hard I struggled letting her into my life, and, quite frankly, there are times it's still a struggle. Now, she thinks I should embrace the whole country."

"Maybe going back will set you free to move forward."

Thai sat in one of his two kitchen chairs. He rested his head in his hands. "I can't," he said in a quiet, pain-filled voice. "I just can't."

"I know going would be hard. . ."

He swallowed. "It would be more than hard."

"At least pray. What if this is more a God thing than a Kinsy thing? What if He's orchestrating these circumstances?"

"I have my doubts." Thai opened his sliding glass door and stepped out on his balcony. Crisp, cool April air blew lightly against his heated cheeks. The sun lingered low in the western sky; in Vietnam, the sun would be rising soon. But Thai's heart was filled with inky darkness.

"So you really liked her, huh?" Thai didn't miss Tong's tactful change of subject. Tong always hit Thai between the eyes with something difficult and just left the seed to germinate. He never nagged or harped, only subtly sowed a kernel of an idea, and left Thai alone to grapple over the issue.

Thai looked at the smoggy sky. "I liked her—a lot. And

her betrayal hurts, man."

"Are you sure this isn't a resolvable misunderstanding?"

Thai told him about his intent to reconcile and about the contents of the letter.

"Sometimes things aren't as they seem. Don't you remember with Lola and me, we had a few miscommunications? I thought one thing, and she thought another."

"Very different. This stared me in the face in black and white. I read the letter. No misunderstanding; believe me the thing would stand up in a court of law. Besides all that—it's like this whole episode has reminded me of just how opposite Kinsy and I are. She wants to embrace Vietnam, and when all the dust settles, I still want to run from it."

"So, what now?"

"I'm going to go talk to her dad—explain why I can't go. If he asks for my resignation, I'll type it for him. Can I crash on your couch for a while if I become unemployed and homeless?" He hoped to lighten Tong's concern.

"You know you can. I'll be praying, and, Thai, you do the same."

He sighed. "I will." The niggling doubt resurfaced. Would God require him to return to Vietnam? The whole notion made him want to shut Kinsy out all the more.

"You can't leave California yet. Samantha is set on visiting Uncle Thai and Mickey come June. You wouldn't break the heart of a three-year-old, would you?"

"Never! Give her a hug from her favorite uncle."

"I will. Love you, bro."

"Back at you." Thai hit the end button on his cordless. Returning inside, he replaced the phone in its cradle and picked up his mail from his tiny table for two. Settling into his recliner, he unmuted the TV, flipped through his mail, and yelled at the Bulls for allowing another turnover.

This place definitely had the look of a bachelor pad. His living room had a recliner, a nice stereo system, and of course, a TV. The stark white walls cried for a decorator's touch, but no decorators lurked on his horizon.

He tried to ignore what Tong had said, but as usual, he couldn't forget. He just hated Tong's ability to calmly place a thorn of doubt in the midst of all his notions. If only Tong would nag, shutting him out would prove an easy task. Instead, he made these profound statements and prayed they'd take root. The words swarmed around and round in Thai's head. *What if this is more a God thing than a Kinsy thing? What if He's orchestrating these circumstances?* And on the heels of these questions, the old memories flooded Thai anew—recollections of a tormented four-year-old who might never find peace.

seven

Kinsy stomped up the steps to her apartment, undecided who'd made her the maddest, Thai, herself, or the driver who just cut her off. The aroma of something Italian and wonderful hit her the minute she unlocked the front door.

"You look like you had a day. Good thing I fixed Chicken Parmesan," Danielle said.

"I did have a day. If my favorite meal can't make me feel better, nothing can." Kinsy glanced at the table. "Candles, linen napkins, fresh flowers and six places set. . ." *Please, God, tell me we're not having a dinner party.* A knock at the door confirmed her suspicions. Kinsy glanced down at her jogging attire and sent Danielle a the-least-you-could-have-done-is-told-me look.

"Would you get it?" Danielle smiled sweetly. "I'm busy with the salad."

Kinsy mentally added Danielle to the list of people who'd annoyed her today. She swung open the front door, and her jaw dropped. "Thai, Rob, Chuck!" Danielle's name just moved to the very top of the list of today's annoyances.

"Aren't you going to invite us in?" Rob asked.

She opened the door wider and Rob led the three of them into the apartment. He carried a bouquet of mixed flowers. Thai's tortured expression left her in no doubt he'd rather be in the hospital with gangrene than here. Somehow he'd been tricked into this little adventure, of that she had no doubt.

"Aren't you going to introduce us?" Rob asked, looking pointedly at Danielle working in the kitchen.

Idiot, she chided herself. She'd stood in the doorway, gaping, as if she didn't have a manner in the world. "Rob, this is my roommate Danielle. Danielle, Rob."

Danielle gave him a bashful grin. "Nice to meet you."

"You, too." Was Rob blushing? "I brought these for you." He held out the flowers.

Certain she'd missed some major clue as to the unfolding of these events, Kinsy shot Danielle a questioning look. Chuck stepped forward, "Danielle, I'm Chuck and this is Thai. I speak for the three of us when I tell you how much we appreciate you inviting us for a home cooked meal." He glanced at Thai. "Well, at least I speak for two of us."

Danielle invited them? Why?

Kally walked through the front door, carrying an armload of books and a filled-to-capacity book bag slung over her shoulder. Her eyes widened upon spotting their dinner guests. "Hello," she said, looking at Kinsy with raised eyebrows as if to say, *What's going on?* Then Kally looked at her attire and Kinsy noticed her lips quiver. She almost laughed!

"Kally," Kinsy said in an artificially sweet voice. "I'd like you to meet Thai. You already know Chuck and Rob. Thai, this is Kally, sister number three."

"Nice to meet you, Thai." Kally smiled then nodded at the other two.

"Danielle, dear," Kinsy continued in her carefully modulated tone. "How long before dinner? Since I've been caught by surprise, I'm hoping I'll have time to shower."

Danielle had the decency to look guilty. "Go ahead."

"Kally, may I help you carry those into your room?" Kinsy asked, taking the stack of books from her. Kally followed her down the hall. The minute they were in Kally's room, Kinsy shut the door. "I have no idea what's going on here, but the timing stinks."

Kally started laughing. "Glad to see you dressed for the occasion."

"This is not funny." Tears came from nowhere. "Our trip is to Vietnam, and Thai hates me." She sat on the edge of Kally's bed, wiping her eyes. The emotions she'd held tight all day threatened to burst forth. "We're through."

Kally sat next to her, putting a comforting arm around her shoulders. She hugged her and never said I told you so, making Kinsy grateful. Finally Kally said, "Run and shower. You'll feel better. I'll entertain the troops."

"Would you bring me my briefcase? I need to make a phone call."

Kinsy slipped into her room and took a fast shower. Then after she threw on jeans and a sweatshirt, she called Steve.

"Hi, Steve, this is Kinsy McCoy."

"Hello, Kinsy. I assume you got my voice mail. You must be thrilled with the news. Vietnam, here she comes! Your dream come true."

Kinsy sighed. Under any other circumstances, she would be thrilled, but her dream wasn't worth Thai. She'd thought about the whole ordeal all day. She wished for a chance at forever with him. This trip would ruin any possibility, if it hadn't already.

"Kinsy, are you there?" Steve's voice brought her out of her reverie.

"Yeah, I'm sorry. I need you to reassign our team. We

can't go to 'Nam." She lay on her back across her bed, staring at the ceiling.

"Too late. We've already purchased the plane tickets in each team member's name. We bought them today, as soon as your secretary E-mailed the list of participants."

"There's no way?" Her words rang with desperation. She laid her hand across her forehead.

"I'm sorry, Kinsy, there's not. I thought you'd be thrilled. You said there was nothing more important than finding your mother's people."

That was then. Now Thai seemed more important. "True, but I ran into a problem on this end. Don't worry. It'll work itself out," she said in a hollow voice.

"Well, have a good evening then."

Saying good-bye, Kinsy didn't know whether to laugh or cry. She had an evening ahead of her all right, but the good part seemed doubtful.

❧

Thai sat stiffly on Kinsy's sofa, staring at the TV, but not really watching the game. Seeing her, being here, brought extreme discomfort. Rob and Chuck had shown up at his doorstep, uninvited and unannounced. He knew better than to leave with them, but he had no idea they'd bring him here. Having heard about the quarrel, they said they came to take him out for a bite, get his mind off his misery. When they pulled up here, he'd almost stayed in the car. However, sitting alone with his memories appealed less than facing Kinsy.

Kally and Chuck both watched the game with him. Rob stayed in the dining area, keeping Danielle company. From the smell of things, he'd at least get a decent meal out of this miserable evening. He wondered where Kinsy was. Maybe she was dolling herself up to make the grand, breathtaking entrance. No matter how good she might look, his decision wouldn't be swayed one iota.

When Kinsy came back in, he didn't even look up. His nose, however, verified her presence by the apple blossom scent of her shampoo. He had no choice but to notice her when she padded barefoot across the blue living room carpet between him and his game. She sat cross-legged in the armchair.

"Dinner's ready," Danielle announced.

Kally flicked off the TV.

Chuck protested.

"Dad says TV has no place at the dinner table. It stifles conversation," Kally informed him.

Thai ended up seated across from Kinsy. He'd been wrong about her dressing to kill. She did just the opposite. She wore a gray sweatshirt, no makeup, and damp hair. She'd been crying. *Probably for my benefit,* he reminded himself after a pang of regret hit his heart. He'd have to stay on his toes.

In all honesty, she left him vulnerable, with an aching need to fill the lonely life he'd carved out for himself. And that vulnerability had made him pretend that his past might not affect them. But Thai had been wrong. Dead wrong. Their first fight had involved the past. Those moments on Half Dome had been nothing more than a surreal removal from reality. Regardless of how he had grown to care for Kinsy, or even his attempts at spiritual growth, she was still Vietnamese. She wanted to embrace her heritage—something Thai could never do. Today's argument had been nothing more than a foretaste of what the future would hold for their relationship.

After Rob said grace, everyone dug in. At least the food was good, even if the atmosphere was strained.

"Danielle, this is delicious," Rob complimented. "Can your roommates cook like this?"

"No," Kinsy and Kally answered in unison.

"We work out the details, though," Kally said. "We buy the groceries and Danielle figures out what to do with them."

Rob chuckled. "I'd be willing to buy, if you'd cook for me."

Danielle smiled and blushed. Kinsy had been right. Danielle did seem perfect for Rob, and the chemistry between them nearly sizzled, just like it had between him and Kinsy.

Dinner passed in small talk. Neither he nor Kinsy said much. Apparently, Kally and Chuck were old friends, and they carried the conversation with tales from high school.

After everyone devoured their homemade cheesecake, they played Rock, Paper, Scissors for cleanup. Thai and Kinsy lost. They cleared the table in silence, avoiding accidentally bumping each other in the small kitchen. When he'd loaded the last plate in the dishwasher, Kinsy had just finished wiping off the table. She stood between him and the kitchen exit.

She swallowed hard. "Can we talk?"

They faced each other, and tension clenched his fists. "There's not much to say."

Her lip quivered. "Please." She barely whispered the word.

"All right," he agreed. Part of him longed to hold her and promise things would be okay, but could they ever be?

"Do you want to walk, so we have some privacy?"

"Lead on."

Thai followed her out the door. She led him to a grassy area under a big oak tree. She sat down, pulling her knees up near her chin. He settled next to her, keeping some distance.

"I'm sorry. I know how this looks to you, but I didn't set out to hurt you." Sad brown eyes pleaded for his understanding. "I know you read the letter on my desk, and the way it's worded sounds incriminating, but that's not exactly what happened."

He didn't say anything. He just stared at her, wondering how he could voice his own jumbled thoughts.

"Thai, please believe me. Yes, when I first talked to Steve—almost a year ago—I shared with him my desire to return to Vietnam one day. When he mentioned 'Nam as one of the Bible smuggling destinations, I said our team would be more than willing to participate."

She paused, apparently waiting for a reaction. With his jaw clenched tight, he had none.

She continued, "That was last fall, before you ever came into the picture. He and I both committed to pray about where God would have this team to go. I should have called him immediately last January when you told me how you felt about Vietnam, but I didn't. I just figured since everyone was praying, God would take care of the details, and I thought if we ended up there maybe you could find freedom and healing from your past."

He resented her pat answers to his childhood pain. The only thing Thai needed freedom and healing from was her. He disliked Christians who blamed God rather than taking responsibility for their own actions. He maintained the cool stare. "You knew about this at Yosemite, didn't you?"

She squirmed under his unyielding scrutiny. "Maybe in my fervor, I forgot to let God be God. I'm sorry. I never meant to hurt you. I should have been more up front with both you and Steve. As Kally frequently reminds me, I have a habit of running about a mile ahead of God and His will for my life." Her eyes glistened with the tears brimming in them.

"I tried not to worry about what would happen between us if Vietnam ended up being our assignment. Anyway, when I learned our destination, I knew you'd be unhappy, but I didn't know you'd end up hating me." She looked away, taking a deep breath.

"Kinsy, I don't hate you. I–I guess I'm just disappointed that you weren't completely honest."

The threatening tears now rolled freely down her cheeks. "I said I was sorry." Her pain-filled eyes made him wonder for a brief moment if he were off base.

"But you never answered my question. You knew at Yosemite, didn't you?"

She nodded and bit her trembling lip.

"Yet you let me kiss you anyway." He shook his head.

"I–I was afraid you'd be angry."

"Angry? If that's all you were afraid of, then—"

"I didn't—didn't realize this would completely jeopardize our relationship. I guess I was naive." She rested her forehead against her knees. "I found your card in my garbage." Her gaze returned to him. "I guess you decided our relationship was over when you learned the complete truth?" Bitterness dripped from each word.

Thai rubbed the base of his neck. "I think it's all bigger than just this deal with the trip," he muttered, realizing he hadn't been exactly honest with Tong either. Thai had placed more of the blame on Kinsy for their breakup than where blame should squarely rest—with his continual struggles with the past.

"It's still all about my being Vietnamese, isn't it?" she rasped.

"Yeah. Afraid so."

"You said at Yosemite you couldn't make me any promises. . . ."

"Yes. And I'm beginning to see that, no matter how attracted I am to you that there's just too much to overcome. You want to embrace Vietnam—"

"And you don't, and you don't want to be close to anyone who does."

Thai examined the grass between them.

Amidst new sniffles, she rose and walked back to her apartment.

He waited a full fifteen minutes before following and was relieved to find Rob and Chuck in the doorway, saying their good-byes. Thai decided to wait at the bottom of the stairs. He should go up and thank Danielle for dinner, but he didn't relish facing Kinsy again tonight.

Rob bounded down the stairs two at a time, his face covered with a mile-wide grin. Thai recognized the symptoms. The falling was great, but the thud when a guy hit bottom left too many bruises.

"Wow, can she cook! A man could get used to her real quick." Rob patted his stomach, stopping on the bottom step.

"But she's not a blond bimbo, Rob. Kinsy says those are more your type." Thai let the sarcasm fly, wondering if Rob's disappointment would hit as quickly as his had.

"Speaking of Kinsy," Rob studied Thai, "What did you

do to her? She came back from your walk sobbing. Went straight to her room. A little early in the relationship for those kind of tears, wouldn't you say? You two should still be in the honeymoon period." Rob headed toward the car.

"We're finished." Thai didn't intend on discussing Kinsy with these guys.

"You broke up with her?" Rob persisted.

Thai nodded, planning to skip any explanation, but Rob's questioning glance prodded him on. "We aren't right for each other."

"Seemed pretty right to me," Rob stated.

"Sometimes reality is different than it seems."

❧

Thai's stony expression had crushed Kinsy. Now, sitting in the middle of her bed, she blotted away the final tears and wondered if she knew him at all. The closing of the front door brought Kinsy out of her room and she glared at Danielle. "What was that I just sat through?" she demanded, her voice grumpier than intended.

"A dinner party." Danielle guiltily shifted in Kinsy's favorite chair.

Hands on her hips, Kinsy challenged, "You just decided out of the blue to invite three guys you've never met over for dinner—one of them being my ex-boyfriend."

Danielle sighed. "Yes, for your own good. Rob called and said you planned on getting the two of us together—"

"I mentioned that to Thai, but I never said a thing to Rob." Kinsy paced to the other side of the room.

"Well apparently Thai did. Anyway, he suggested tonight might be a good night because you and Thai had a spat. He hoped to give you two a chance to make up. Since I'm off on Mondays, the plans worked out fine."

"They did?" A bitter chuckle escaped her lips. Kinsy let out a sigh and dropped onto the sofa. "I'm sorry. You're not the enemy, and I know you tried to help."

"I'm sorry, too. I shouldn't have meddled," Danielle said, flicking off the TV with the remote.

"Your heart was right. It's just been a lousy day." Beyond weary, Kinsy buried her face in her hands.

"Thai seems nice enough. What happened?"

"I told him this morning our summer trip is to Vietnam. He thinks I arranged the destination—which I guess I did, at least in part. Then, he found out I didn't tell him at Yosemite. It all looks really bad." She sighed. "But the bottom line is that he can't get past his past and he sees me as a representative of the whole thing."

"I thought he was moving away from all that."

"Yeah, me, too." Kinsy didn't want to discuss Thai anymore. Just thinking about him depressed her. "What's your opinion of Rob?"

Danielle's face lit up. "I liked him."

"It appeared the feeling was mutual. Where's Kally?"

"In her room grading her stack of papers."

"I need to call my dad. I'll see you in the morning. Thanks for trying, but next time will you clue me in?"

Danielle nodded, and the two friends exchanged an all-is-well-between-us smile.

Back in her room, Kinsy hit number one on her speed dial. "Hi, Daddy, it's me. I need to let you know things have worsened with Thai. Can I ask Rob to replace him on the trip?"

"Do what you think best."

"Okay," she appreciated his confidence in her. "Thai's not ready to face Vietnam. I see that now. I talked to Steve, and it's too late to change our itinerary. Maybe Rob can clear his schedule and come."

"Fine. Let Thai know he's off the hook, with my blessing. I don't want him to worry about any fallout from this.

"Thanks, Daddy."

"You sound low. Has this affected your relationship with Thai?"

Kinsy tried to swallow the lump in her throat. She answered with a strained, "Yes."

"I'm sorry, Pumpkin. I wish I could make everything work out, but Thai's a smart man. He'll figure things out in time, but I'm sure he's struggling right now. Give him a little space."

"I will. Thanks."

"Sleep well."

"You, too."

Certain all was lost between her and Thai, Kinsy began to accept that he had indeed used her as a guinea pig and that the experiment had failed. No matter what the future held, Thai wouldn't be a part of her life. Acknowledging the truth didn't make the bearing any easier. She'd lost her heart to a man who viewed her as everything he needed to avoid.

eight

Thai hadn't slept well. He'd almost taken a day off, but what for? To sit around brooding about yesterday? Not too appealing. He thought maybe work would take his mind off the rest of his life, but here he sat, and yesterday hung around him like a dark cloak.

He walked to the window. The sunshine didn't dispel his gloom. He returned to his desk just as Kinsy stuck her head into his office.

"Do you have a minute?" she asked.

At his nod, she came in and pushed the door closed. Tell-tale circles peeked from under her eyes. Even though he didn't plan to, he reacted at the sight of her—first with a pleasurable rush and then with a disappointed pang.

She sat in one of the two burgundy padded chairs across from his desk.

"What do you need, Kinsy?" he asked, more abruptly than he'd intended.

She looked down at her hands, folded in her lap. She drew her lips together in a tight line. For a moment, he thought she might cry.

Then she looked him straight in the eye. "You're off the hook. I found someone else to accompany us on the trip. My dad said to tell you you're appreciated and respected. This will in no way affect your position here at CC or reflect on your record."

He nodded his acknowledgment. Guilt stabbed him in

the midsection. He'd wrestled with God all night about this decision. Now free to back out, he wasn't sure what to do.

Kinsy rose to leave. She stopped halfway between the door and the chair she'd just vacated, and turning back to face him, she said, "I'm sorry, Thai. For everything. Please believe me." She didn't even try to hide the anguish in her voice. Her eyes shined with unshed tears.

He looked away, hands gripping the edge of his desk, fighting the urge to go to her. "Kinsy. . ." He glanced up, but she was gone. The rest of his sentence died on his tongue.

In the aftermath of that encounter, Thai decided to talk to Karl; after all, he was not only his boss but also his spiritual shepherd. Of course, he was also Kinsy's father. Thai entered the small alcove where Karl's secretary sat behind her desk. She buzzed Karl and sent Thai right in.

Karl rose from behind his desk, came around it, and shook Thai's hand. Then he and Thai each sat in the two straight-backed chairs.

"Kinsy gave me your message. Thank you," Thai said. He appreciated the compassion on Karl's face.

"I'm sorry this happened. My Kinsy-girl is a selfless person who really does love God with her whole heart. In her fervor, she sometimes plows ahead and runs over a few toes."

Thai's toes were more intact than his crushed heart. "I know she longs to go back so much, she can't understand my hesitancy to face my worst nightmare again. I thought I was clear with her about my never returning. I don't understand why she did this to me." He shook his head.

"She means well, Thai. She really does. She gets an idea and runs straight ahead. Convinced facing your demons would free you, she hoped you'd go for your own sake."

"I know, but that's my decision to make. I may never feel the way she does about my Asian heritage."

Karl nodded. "You're right and she was wrong. She admits it. Her tendency is to embrace everything about life and expect others to do the same. She hasn't walked in your shoes, so she can't know your pain. Kinsy's had an easy life. Adopted as a baby, no memories of the war, she grew up with love and acceptance." Deep wisdom shone from Karl's eyes.

"I appreciate your understanding." Thai already held the graying minister in high esteem and he just moved up a notch.

"From the discussions I've had with Kinsy, I know she now realizes the error of her ways," Karl said. "In her excitement to finally fulfill her long-held dream, she figured God provided a great opportunity for you as well, so she didn't mention any of this to Steve, thinking she left the whole situation in God's hands. I don't believe she intended to deceive you, but I know she pushed you between a rock and a cliff."

Thai sighed. "She sure did. I just don't want this to affect my relationship with you, the rest of the staff, or my job in any way."

"I assure you, it won't. I've spent almost three decades reminding Kinsy to slow down and practice patience. She's learning, but like all of us, has room to grow. I do think you should know she tried to give up her dream for your sake."

"What do you mean?" Thai asked.

"When Steve announced the destination, she immediately called him to get the itinerary changed. By then, she realized she'd rather lay down her dream than put you in a spot you weren't ready to be in."

Surprised, Thai asked, "She did?"

Karl nodded. "Unfortunately, too much time had lapsed. The airline tickets were purchased."

"So there's an airline ticket in my name?" Thai had been asking God to confirm His will about this trip, leaning toward being obedient instead of obstinate, if this were indeed more of a God thing than a Kinsy thing. Karl's words brought a stab of confirmation to Thai's heart.

"Don't worry about it though. Kinsy offered to pay for Rob's ticket since she's responsible for the problem. She wouldn't allow the church to bear the financial burden of her mistake."

Great! Thai momentarily wondered if he should call her Saint Kinsy. Yes, she had her flaws, but through Karl's eyes, she seemed pretty special, a selfless woman of integrity. "So Rob's going in my place?"

"He'll know for sure in a couple of days. He's trying to clear his calendar and get everything covered."

"Well, hopefully everything will work out." Thai rose to leave. "Thanks for understanding."

"You're welcome, Thai. Any time." They shook hands.

Thai headed straight for Rob's office, more confident with each step.

"Hey, my man," Thai greeted Rob.

"Thai, so you're still talking to me. After last night I wondered if you'd forgive me for butting into your and Kinsy's relationship."

"Forgiven and forgotten. I know you were only trying to help. Now I need a favor."

"Name it. I guess I owe you big time," Rob replied.

"Will you wait a day before clearing your calendar?"

"Are you thinking about going?"

"I'm experiencing pangs of conviction. I'm spending the rest of the day in prayer and fasting. I don't plan to say anything to anyone else until I'm sure. Especially not Kinsy."

"Does this mean you're going to give her another chance?"

"No, it just means I intend to be certain I'm obeying God. I think Kinsy and I both realize it would never work between us. We're just too different." *And she's still too Asian.* Even if God gave Thai the strength to return to Vietnam, he doubted that he could ever be completely free of his past.

❧

Kinsy drove back to the church after a quick dinner with her roommates. Wednesday evening had arrived and so had their first training for the Vietnam trip. She hadn't seen Thai since yesterday morning, but she had done a lot of soul searching since then.

Thai was right to be disappointed in her. She should have never hidden the truth from him at Yosemite. Finally, Kinsy had admitted that to herself and God. Deep inside, she'd hoped Vietnam would be their ultimate destination. Both her reasons were purely selfish. The first—she wanted to go, plain and simple. The second—she knew in order for her and Thai to have a future, he needed to face his past. How could he ever love her when he had so many hang-ups about the Vietnamese people?

She'd let go of any hope for a future with Thai. Her heart ached, and her only hope was that he would someday forgive her. Even friendship appeared impossible, and maybe too painful.

Kinsy parked her car close to the youth building where

the college, high school, and junior high classrooms were located. Tonight she and Rob were meeting with the team of ten to start their training. She grabbed her briefcase and walked to the correct room. No one had arrived yet. Placing twelve chairs in a circle, she then laid a handout on each one. The team trickled in one or two at a time. At seven o'clock, Kinsy decided to go ahead and start. Since Rob was only a stand-in, she'd not given him much responsibility.

Taking one of the two empty chairs within the circle, she introduced herself and then each of the students introduced themselves. All the faces were familiar except one. Everyone briefly shared what had drawn them to this trip.

Kinsy glanced at her watch. 7:15. *Where's Rob?* She decided she might as well break the news: Thai wouldn't be part of the team. "Thai—"

"Is running late and apologizes," he blurted, rushing through the door and taking the last chair in the circle. "Tonight I thought I'd share an overview about Vietnam, after Kinsy explains what she needs to about the packets."

Kinsy's mouth fell open. Shock, surprise, amazement, and disbelief all shot through her. Where was the angry, hurt guy she'd left yesterday morning? This fellow looked like a man without a care in the world. He wore his favorite Bears T-shirt and a Bulls cap, and her heart reacted with a painful longing.

"Kinsy? Are you with us?" he asked, lifting his eyebrows.

"Sorry. I guess my mind wandered." She had lost her focus and forgotten her entire mental agenda for this meeting. "Tell you what, why don't you take the floor? I can cover the packets next week. Everyone take them home and study the information. We'll discuss any questions at our next meeting."

They all nodded their agreement.

Thai took over. "Most of the Vietnamese are Buddhists who desperately need Jesus. An underground church meets in homes. Hungry for God's Word, they tear a Bible into many sections, so each person can have a few chapters to read. Then they trade them back and forth, reading them so often they wear out in no time. The point of our trip is to supply the church with more Bibles.

"We'll leave LAX, change planes at Tokyo's Narita International Airport, and end up at the Tan Son Nhut airport in Ho Chi Minh City, better known as Saigon. Pack light because of the Bibles. We're allowed three large suitcases apiece. Two and a half of them will be filled with Bibles, leaving half of a suitcase for all your personal effects."

Kinsy watched Thai, amazed at his metamorphosis. *What was he doing here and what in the world changed his mind?* He'd apparently studied all the information thoroughly and paid attention to what she'd previously shared.

"We'll actually only leave the airport with the one suitcase—the one filled with half Bibles and half clothes. The other two will be whisked away to places unknown. We're traveling under the guise of a humanitarian aid trip, and our home base will be an orphanage, run by a Christian couple, and situated about ten miles outside of Saigon.

"They'll provide us with cyclos, better known as bikes. Those will be our transportation to visit small villages in the vicinity, under the guise of sightseeing. While in those villages, we'll connect with the contact person for the underground church and bless them with the Bibles."

Kamie's best friend, Lindsay, raised her hand. Her pale

blond hair would definitely earmark her as a foreigner. "What would happen if we got caught delivering the Bibles?"

"We are in little danger," Thai assured them. "But the Vietnamese receiving the Bibles could be in grave danger, even face a prison sentence. So we need to present ourselves as model tourists and be wise and careful, for their sakes."

Everyone nodded their understanding.

"My dad said it's really hot there."

"He's right, Justin. The humidity and temperature run neck and neck, so a ninety-degree day with ninety percent humidity isn't uncommon. The summers are hot and wet—wet with rain and soggy with humidity."

"Are you from Vietnam, Thai?" asked Kristen.

"Originally." He glanced at Kinsy and she knew the horrors still plagued him. "As are Kinsy and Kamie."

"Do any of you remember the country at all?" Melissa asked, her almost black hair pulled back into a ponytail.

"I have some memories." Thai paused, pain flashed in his eyes. "I don't think Kamie or Kinsy remember anything. Right, ladies?"

Both nodded.

"Tell us about it and your life there. Maybe share a favorite memory." Kristen requested.

Thai glanced at Kinsy. He'd gone slightly ashen, but he recovered quickly. She wondered if he had any favorite memories.

He cleared his throat and began, "I was almost four. My family lived in the coastal fishing town of Phan Thiet. My father, uncles, grandfather, and many generations before them were fishermen. Year 'round the smell of fish hung in the air. When my mother, brother Loi, and I moved to Saigon, I missed the aroma of fish almost as much as I missed our family. For me it had been the smell of home. Fourteen of us lived in Grandma's house, a warm place filled with laughter and love.

"Anyway, this memory sticks in my head. Loi, our five cousins, and I walked down the shady avenue from Grandma's toward a kiosk resting under an old tamarind tree. Our sandals crunched on the sand as we went. We all held hands and sang." A faraway look stole over Thai's face. "I was the baby of the group. I remember thinking life just didn't get any better than that. I felt safe, loved, and protected. We each bought a breadfruit milkshake."

He paused and Kinsy thought she caught sight of the glimmer of tears in his eyes. "A week later, all of them but me, Mama, and Loi were dead." The wooden words held no expression or tone, and the muscle in Thai's jaw tightened.

Everyone in the room gasped and then a silence fell over them. Kinsy longed to comfort him in some way, but knew only God could really heal and comfort Thai.

"I'm sorry. I didn't mean to shock you. I guess part of our going is facing the pain and destruction this country faced. Some of the people will hate you because you're American. Many believe America deserted them before the war was finished. Most have lived through loss, pain, and devastation. The more you know about their past, the more compassion and care you can show the people."

Amidst respectful silence, Kinsy distributed some Vietnamese language tapes for the team and encouraged them to begin learning the language. After a few more questions, the first training session ended.

Everyone left, and Kinsy gathered her belongings. Thai

filed the paperwork in his briefcase. Words of comfort filled her mind, but she had no idea what to say or not to say. She longed to take his hand in hers, squeeze it with compassion, and offer tender expressions of sympathy, but remembering his rejection the last time she reached for him stopped her.

Even "I'm glad you changed your mind might" lead him to believe she gloated, though gloating was the last thing on her mind. There was nothing she regretted more than the pain she'd caused Thai because of this trip. So in silence, they worked side by side returning the chairs to their original places.

❧

Although Kinsy toiled near Thai, hundreds of miles emotionally separated them. When the room was neat and tidy, they shut out the lights and walked outside. Overwrought, Thai didn't have the strength to explain how he ended up here at the meeting or why he was suddenly back on the team. Instead, he simply said, "I guess I'll see you next Wednesday."

"Guess, so," she agreed. Her lip quivered, but she kept her chin high, not giving in to the tears shimmering in her eyes.

The night ended. Kinsy turned right and walked down the sidewalk toward the north parking lot without looking back. She'd not said a thing, though he'd seen a million questions in her eyes. She was hurting. He was hurting, and it didn't appear either would get better. He headed toward his car in the south lot.

During his prayer and fasting yesterday, he finally accepted facts. God desired for him to face his past, and He wasn't going to let Thai rest easy until he did. Both

Kinsy and Tong were right. Sometimes you have to look back before you're free to move into the future. Ready for God to heal him, he knew healing included pain.

He also realized the next couple of months would be the hardest of his life, but once he'd decided to go on this trip, peace flooded his soul. Choosing God's will instead of his own way empowered him. He would get through this, but he needed all his focus and energy on God. He refused to be diverted by Kinsy and his conflicting emotions in regard to her.

nine

Throngs of passengers crowded the terminals at LAX the morning of their departure for Vietnam. Thai arrived early, finding the designated meeting place by the ticket counter where they could all check in together. Tong, Lola, and their two children had been visiting for a week and insisted on accompanying him. They wouldn't be flying out for a couple more days and planned to take the kids down to Sea World today after Thai left.

Fascinated by the large, rolling suitcases, one-year-old Thomas held on to them and used them to navigate. He wasn't quite ready to trek off on his own yet. Uncertain whether or not she wanted to be awake this early, three-year-old Sammy sat quietly on Lola's lap.

Thai didn't know for certain if he wanted to be awake this early either. The closer the trip grew, the more nightmares had disrupted his sleep, and last night he'd barely dozed. He spent much of the night in prayer, trying to take captive his thoughts. He reminded himself over and over that God did not give him a spirit of fear.

He spotted Kinsy coming. Both Kally and Danielle were with her. He rose to help them with the suitcases and recalled the final understanding in her eyes when she met Lola and saw how her blond features produced children who weren't strongly Asian. At last she seemed to understand Thai's cry for a blond wife, and the emotional wall between them had grown all the thicker. Except for the training sessions, Thai had avoided her. Yet all night thoughts of Kinsy had mingled with his Vietnam past. . . holding Kinsy, kissing Kinsy, everything about Kinsy.

As he approached them, he noticed her tired eyes. She must not be sleeping well, either. They didn't see him because they were laughing and struggling with the big heavy suitcases.

"Let me help you with those, ladies," Thai offered. Tong was right behind him to carry another one. Kinsy's smile vanished the moment she saw him. All emotion left her eyes, as if she'd closed the door of her soul against him.

Thai and Tong each carried one of the large cases back to their destination. The three women managed to tug and slide the last suitcase to the growing pile before Thai could get back to help them.

Thai introduced Kinsy's roommates to his family. The team began drifting in, and Thai and Tong helped with the heavy suitcases. Just as Thai and Tong had rounded up all thirty-six suitcases, Karl and Kettie arrived. Thai checked the suitcases with the porter and gathered everyone. Family and friends accompanied each of the team members, and they created a large huddle.

"Karl plans to share a few parting words with us," Thai announced.

"We're here to dedicate each member of this team to the Lord. May each fulfill the special work He's planned for him. Just like the believers in Acts, I'd like us to lay hands on them, pray for them, and send them on their way."

The team formed a tight circle, with intertwined arms. Everyone moved closer around them, placing their hands on the travelers' backs and shoulders. Peace washed over Thai's weary soul.

After prayer time, everyone said their good-byes to friends and family members. Thai, overwhelmed with uncertainties, hugged his brother tightly. "I love you, Tong."

"I know."

"I still miss Loi, but I'm so grateful God gave me you for a little brother."

Tong hugged him back. "And I love you, Thai. I'll be praying. I sense God's going to do a great work in you while you're there."

"I sense that, too, and it terrifies me." Thai chuckled. "I'm not sure why I always dread God's scalpel. After the pain of His surgery, the blessings flow. I just hate the pain."

"Don't we all," Tong said.

Thai bid farewell to his sister-in-law, niece, and nephew, then Karl was his last good-bye.

"I'll be praying for each of you by name," Karl promised, first shaking Thai's hand and then hugging him. "Especially you."

"Thanks, Karl." Thai appreciated his sensitivity.

Thai took an index card from his pocket and called out each name, "Kamie, Lindsay, Melissa, Kim, Kristen, Daniel, Eddie, Justin, Nick, Nate, and Kinsy, it's time." His gaze drifted over each face; the excitement and anticipation he saw warmed his heart. He sensed the Lord's presence with them, and God's peace filled Thai's soul.

"Time to get our boarding passes." They all turned for one last wave to their loved ones standing nearby. Thai smiled at Tong. With his arm around Lola, he held her close to his side. Thai looked forward to the day he had a Lola in his life. Kinsy caught his eye as she ran back to give Kally a last hug. He almost wished she'd been the one.

"Kally is moving to Phoenix to take care of an elderly

lady who is like a second mother to her." As they walked toward the security booth, Thai strained to catch Kamie's every word. "Kally lived with her while she was in college. The lady has cancer now and doesn't have a soul to help her. Kally will be gone before we get back. She and Kinsy are very close since they've lived together the past three years. On top of that, Danielle—their other roommate—is getting married."

"Poor Kinsy," Lindsay said with sympathy.

After they passed through security and obtained their boarding passes, they claimed the vacant chairs in the waiting area. Kinsy stood on the other side of the room, and Thai gazed toward the planes on the runway, trying to convince himself that he was better off with Kinsy out of sight. But Thai soon found himself rising and approaching her against the demands of his common sense.

❧

The airport waiting area was crowded. Kinsy made certain all the participants were seated with at least one other member of the team. Then she found an empty chair herself. She closed her eyes. Kally's moving to Phoenix troubled her. Telling her sister good-bye proved difficult. She didn't want to think about her future or Kally's. Both probably faced a tough year.

"Mind if I sit here?" Thai's voice broke into Kinsy's thoughts.

She opened her eyes and there he stood, looking uncertain as to what her reaction might be. She shrugged. "Suit yourself." She slid as far to the other edge of her chair as she could.

"I heard Kamie say Danielle is engaged."

Kinsy nodded, not even looking in Thai's direction,

hoping he'd get the hint. She wasn't interested in idle chatter. The farther away from her he stayed, the happier she'd be.

"Rob?"

Again, she only nodded.

"Wow! He didn't even tell me! They moved quick didn't they?"

"I guess when you meet the right person, it doesn't take long to figure it out." Thoughts of her and Thai's rocky relationship twisted her words with bitterness.

"And Kally's moving to Phoenix to take care of a friend?"

"For awhile."

A man's voice came over the speaker announcing the boarding of their flight. Thai stood, and their ten charges gathered round.

"Let's move over to a corner for some last minute reminders," Thai said.

He looked like a mama hen with all her chicks trailing behind. Kinsy brought up the rear.

Thai spoke quietly, so they all surrounded him in a tight circle. "Remember, when we land in Vietnam, Kinsy will lead us through customs. We don't want to give the appearance we're traveling as a group, so mingle with the other passengers. Spread out going through immigration. Don't talk to or look at each other. That's why all our suitcases look very different, so if they catch one, they hopefully won't catch us all."

"What would happen if we got caught going through customs?" Concern laced Kamie's question. Her face paled a shade or two.

"Don't worry. Like I already told you, they'll just confiscate your luggage. Remember, we are more of a threat to the people we meet than to ourselves. We'll just pray our way through. Determine to look and act natural and pray all the way."

As their rows were called for boarding, they all made their way to the gate. After storing her backpack in the overhead bin, Kinsy sat with Kamie and Lindsay. Thai took the seat directly behind her, next to Eddie and Daniel.

"Thai, what happened to your mom and brother?" Eddie asked.

"They were killed in an explosion."

"Where were you?"

He sighed. "Down the block, watching it happen." Pain filled his words, and Kinsy cringed. At last, she had gotten what she wanted. Thai was facing his past. Now, Kinsy wasn't sure if she'd be strong enough to go back to the scene of such devastation.

"How horrible. Sorry, man."

"Me, too," the other participant said.

"Hey, let's find another subject," Thai injected with false cheerfulness. "Did you guys see the game last night?"

The conversation took off on sports. Kinsy quit listening. The engines revved up and the plane started rolling away from the terminal. They taxied to the runway and waited in line for takeoff.

Her mind returned to Thai. Everything she learned about him only made her love him more. He'd been through so much. *God, please give him a happy life filled with Your blessings. . .and a wife, Lord, a good wife as well. He deserves someone who will understand him far better than I have.*

The plane sped down the runway. Its nose lifted and Kinsy asked God to hold them in His righteous right hand.

Her heart beat a little faster. She was going home!

❧

The sports conversation died, and Thai closed his eyes in an attempt to catch up on his sleep. Yet the memories began to play out in slow motion. *Take captive my thoughts,* he reminded himself, only to have his thoughts roam toward Kinsy. Something deep within him yearned for them to find a peace with each other. Her eyes assured him that she was hurting as much as he was. Thai sighed, punched the little pillow he'd received from the stewardess, and tried to find a comfortable position. He prayed about Kinsy and promised God he'd at least offer a token of friendship. Kinsy was special and deserved someone better than a man whose past marred his present.

Thai somehow managed to get a few hours of exhausted, dreamless sleep before changing flights in Tokyo. By the time Vietnam Airlines Flight 742 touched down in Saigon, his adrenaline pumped, and his exhaustion fled. He was back in Vietnam, whether he wanted to be or not. His stomach knotted, yet he was also excited about delivering the Bibles.

When the fasten seatbelt sign shut off, Kinsy rose and grabbed her backpack and headed into the aisle. She glanced in his direction, and her eyes reflected the same fear and exhilaration he was experiencing. He winked at her, and her eyes widened. As she glanced away, Thai didn't take the time to question his spontaneous gesture. Instead, he hoped and prayed she'd get through customs without a hitch.

A few passengers followed Kinsy down the aisle and then Kamie moved into the crowd waiting to disembark. They continued the process until only Thai remained seated. He stood. It seemed like forever since Kinsy disappeared toward the front of the plane.

Thai continued to pray for each of them as they moved ahead to board the shuttle bus. Thai kept his eye on Eddie, Daniel, and Kristen. They were the only team members in his line of vision. He longed to catch a glimpse of Kinsy and know she was safe.

He nodded and smiled to the stewardesses. Both were Vietnamese, but not nearly as pretty as Kinsy. For the first time, Thai realized, he had looked at Asian women without the stabbing pain searing his heart. He moved quickly toward the shuttle bus that would carry them to the airport. The team members sat exclusively to themselves, never acknowledging that they knew each other. They unloaded and Thai again lost sight of his companions. His heart pounded in anticipation of the unknown lying ahead. He continued to pray, and Kinsy weighed the heaviest on his heart.

The man who cleared his papers was curt. Thai moved on to the baggage claim area. He spotted about half of his team, also awaiting luggage, and caught a glimpse of a few others heading toward the baggage X-ray. Finally Thai's first bag came by, he grabbed it, and loaded it on a cart. After snaring the rest of his luggage, he moved toward the baggage X-ray and prayed all the more fervently as he witnessed each members' bags being cleared. At last he followed the team members to the exit.

When Thai left the airport through the glass doors, humid air, hot and thick, closed in around him. His lungs worked harder, and sweat beaded on his forehead. Traffic noises and voices rang loud as he passed through the wall of waiting people. Off to the left, he spotted the white van which would carry the Bibles to their planned destination.

"You last one? Number twelve?" the driver asked in broken English as Thai approached with his luggage.

"Yes," he replied and the driver heaved the luggage into the van.

Thai smiled. Gratefulness welled up in his chest. The whole dozen of them had safely arrived! *Thanks, Lord, and please enable the rest of the smuggling to go this smoothly.* The driver slammed the van door and crawled behind the steering wheel. Thai watched as the van pulled away from the curb and into traffic. He prayed for each of the almost one thousand Bibles they'd smuggled in. *May each one fall into the hands of a hungry Christian and not into the wrong hands.*

Thai looked around, taking in the sights and sounds of his homeland. A lump rose in his throat. Emotions he'd buried twenty-six years ago bubbled just below the surface. *God, we need You so much. Protect our team. Carry me through the days ahead. Heal my heart. And somehow help me sort through all this confusion over Kinsy.*

He walked across the parking lot, following the directions to where the orphanage van waited to whisk them away. When he spotted the team standing beside the light blue van, he jogged the rest of the way, anxious to hug each one of them.

"We made it!" he stated the obvious. He pulled Nate and Nick into a hug. "We made it!" Relief washed over him, and the apprehension over customs faded into the past.

"Thai," Kinsy said from behind him. He turned and fought the urge to hug her as well. "This is Cadeo and Lan. They run the orphanage." He shook Cadeo's hand and then remembered to bow low. *It's paramount that in your ignorance you don't give offense,* is what the literature Steve had sent to the team said. He also bowed low to greet Lan. They both looked close to his age.

"Welcome, *ban* or friend," Cadeo said in English. "You are most honored guest, and you are also Vietnamese?"

Thai's defenses rose. He almost shouted, I'm an American! Instead he nodded his agreement. He hated that question, but hid his distaste. He'd spent his life correcting people. Now was not the time to continue in that vein.

Cadeo invited Thai to sit in the front of the van with him. "Lan and Kinsy will enjoy visit."

Everyone climbed in, finding a spot. As they pulled out of the airport, Thai's stomach knotted tighter. Things looked familiar, yet unfamiliar. He'd forgotten how green the countryside was. Stray vendors here and there sold food from baskets. Billboards dotted the skyline advertising familiar products like Honda, IBM, and Coca-Cola.

The streets were crazy, people honking, yelling, and making obscene gestures. Most intersections bore no traffic signs or signals, so the right of way went to the most daring and persistent. Thai gripped the handle above his door, praying all the way. "This is nuts," he commented. At each intersection, people, bikes, scooters, jeeps, ox carts, trucks, and animals jockeyed for position.

"We barrel through," Cadeo said confidently, barely missing a woman on a bike.

"Why isn't she wearing a helmet?" Thai asked.

Cadeo chuckled. "People here can't even afford eyeglasses, and you wonder about helmets? They cost sixty American dollars—twice what a teacher earns in a month. It's too hot, anyway. No one would wear them, even if they could afford them. It's not surprising that head injury is the number one cause of death here in the city."

A man on a scooter glared at Cadeo as he fought him for the right of way. Neither backed down and Thai wondered if the man had a brain since their van could mash his scooter into the ground. That made no difference. He insisted on going first, and Cadeo swerved at the last second to avoid flattening him.

The victor moved ahead, already engaged in another battle of the wheels with a taxi. "Driving in Saigon is a contest of the will," Cadeo stated. "It's part of the Vietnamese way of life."

Thai remembered in amazement how he and Loi ran through the crowded streets, only now they seemed more crowded and louder. With painful clarity, he saw two little boys, traipsing through the town like they owned the place. Pain shot through him. *Loi, I miss you so much!* His eyes burned, and swallowing proved impossible.

ten

The van crunched over the gravel drive leading to the old two-story building housing the orphanage. Kinsy's heart pounded. This worn building, or Lan's parents, might hold the key to her past. Anticipation fought with fear. On shaky legs, Kinsy rose from her seat.

Thai offered his hand to help her down. She accepted. His touch sent even more emotions reeling within her. "You okay?" He spoke softly near her ear. His warm breath against her neck caused goose bumps to shoot up her spine.

She disliked needing him, but a part of her longed to collapse against him and let his strength be her own. He tightened his hold on her hand as if he'd read her mind. Kinsy smiled up at him. He blurred slightly, and she swallowed hard.

The slamming of a door brought her attention back to the orphanage. About ten smiling, shouting children bounded toward them. A small girl got knocked down in the process. No one stopped to help her; they just skirted her and kept going until they reached Cadeo.

Thai ran and picked up the crying girl. He held her close and kissed her check. His tenderness touched Kinsy. He said something, and the little girl laughed; her braids bobbed up and down. He carried her toward the van, and she rubbed her eyes with her fists.

"Kinsy, will you hold her while I help Cadeo and the boys with the luggage?" He tried to pass the child to Kinsy, but the little girl wrapped her arms tightly around Thai's neck, refusing to let go.

"Cai, are you okay?" Lan asked.

The little girl nodded.

"Cai, this is Mr. Thai and Miss Kinsy. They've come to help us for a little while."

"Do the children speak English?" Kinsy asked, surprised.

"Since many of them are adopted by families from the U.S., we only speak English here at the orphanage. They learn Vietnamese as a second language when they start school," Lan said.

"Cai, I love your braids," Kinsy told her. The little girl smiled and touched her hair. She was an adorable child—sincere brown eyes, a pug nose, and a rosebud mouth. "Would you like to come show me your house while Mr. Thai carries in my suitcase?"

Cai looked at Thai then back at Kinsy. Kinsy held out her arms. Cai hesitated, looking at Thai again.

"I'll come get you as soon as I'm done," he promised. "Miss Kinsy's a very nice lady." He looked at her with warm eyes.

Kinsy swam in a pool of confusion as his recent wink plagued her memory. *Why are you doing this to me*? she wanted to blurt out. *I thought any chances between us were over*.

Cai finally said, "You can put me down now."

Both Thai and Kinsy laughed. He put her down and squatted at her level. "You're not such a little girl after all. How old are you?" Thai asked.

Cai held up four fingers. "And a half," she added proudly.

"How about a tour while the guys unload?" Lan asked Kinsy.

"Sounds great."

"I'll lead," Cai announced.

"Come on girls and I'll show you around," Lan called. She followed Cai, with Kinsy and the five girls on her heels.

The orphanage, shabby on the outside, was in better shape on the inside than Kinsy expected. They housed about fifty children in two large dorm-type rooms. The children decorated their own spaces. Cai proudly led them to her purple area. She'd painted the wall purple, her quilt was purple with white daisies, and she had a purple dresser.

"I bet I know your favorite color," Kinsy said.

"I like pink, too," Cai informed her. "What color do you like, Miss Kinsy?"

"Pink—definitely pink." She winked at Cai.

"I love the way you've managed to let each child capture his own individuality in a dorm-like setting," Kinsy commented, running her hand over Cai's silky hair.

"I'm just following my mom's lead," Lan said. "She wanted each child to know he was unique and special to God. She helped them find and develop their gifts. I try to do the same."

"Sounds like your mom's a wise lady."

"She is."

"How did you meet Cadeo?" Kinsy asked as they toured the boys' dorm. She loved a good love story.

"He grew up here in the orphanage. I fell in love with him when I was about eight. My mom insisted he must feel the same way, but you couldn't prove it by me. He teased me unmercifully, pulled my pigtails, and hit me every chance he got. Mom said that's how ten-year-old boys show affection.

"He was almost adopted at twelve, by a Canadian couple. I cried myself to sleep every night, begging God not to let him go. A couple of years later I felt horrible and selfish for cheating him out of a family, so I confessed to him what I'd done." Lan's eyes misted over.

"He told me he'd prayed the same prayer. He reached out and gently ran his fingers over my cheek. 'I would have come back for you,' he'd said, and from that day on, I knew he was my soul mate. He never hit me or pulled my hair again. Instead, he started being gentle and thoughtful." Lan grinned. "How about you and Thai? How did your love story begin?"

Kinsy looked at her dirt smudged Keds. "Thai and I aren't. . ."

"I'm sorry. I just assumed," Lan stammered. "I mean the way you two look at each other. Anyway, what do you think of the old place?" Lan asked as they completed the tour.

"It's wonderful," Kinsy said, trying to stifle a yawn.

"You must be exhausted after such a long flight and many time changes."

"I am. It's about three in the morning back home."

"And here it is almost dinner time. Are you hungry?"

Kinsy nodded. Their last plane meal was hours behind her.

Lan stepped outside and rang a large dinner bell. Children came from every direction. Lan led her to a huge room filled with tables and chairs. Along one wall, a counter laden with huge urns of soup, bowls, and spoons beckoned them.

Cadeo and Thai entered with the five boys. Thai's gaze caught hers. He smiled, and her heart responded with gladness. She smiled back, wishing he loved her. As much as she planned to treat him with cool disdain, she couldn't pull it off for more than a few minutes. He walked toward her, Cai's hand in his.

"How's everything?" he asked.

"Fine. How about you?"

"Grab a hand for prayer," Cadeo said loudly over the dull roar of conversation. Thai took Kinsy's, and Kinsy reached for the hand of a little boy about ten. He glared at her, said something hateful in Vietnamese, and moved away. Stunned, Kinsy didn't understand. Then all the children moved away from her, and she recalled the training material mentioning Vietnamese prejudice against Amerasians.

Lan stepped up and took Kinsy's hand, and Cadeo blessed the food. Kinsy didn't hear his words though because she was so hurt by the children's rejection.

"I'm sorry, Kinsy," Lan whispered after Cadeo said amen. "Some of the children have learned prejudices at school. I will have Cadeo speak to them later tonight."

"But I'm half Vietnamese," Kinsy said as if that would somehow end generations of ingrained attitudes.

Thai still held her hand, gently massaging it with his thumb. Through blurred vision, she watched Cai run off and join the other children in line to get her soup. Two young girls spooned the soup into the bowls for the children.

"The problem is you are also part American. Many Vietnamese hate the Americans for leaving us and blame them because we lost the war and our freedom. The children pick up these attitudes from peers and teachers."

"Yes, I know," Kinsy whispered. Somehow she had naively assumed that because she was coming to help, the children would accept her.

❧

Anger sparked in Thai. No one should be so rude to Kinsy.

He thought about grabbing the kid by the scruff of his neck and setting him straight. The hurt clouding her eyes only intensified his protective instincts. Thai wrapped his arm around her shoulders. "Cadeo will take care of it." He led her toward the chow line. "Let's eat. I'm starved."

"Hope you like rice and catfish soup," Lan said from right behind them.

"I think I do," Thai said, as they took their place in line. The smell of the soup caused a memory to surface. He could see his grandmother in her kitchen, cooking for the family. A longing flooded him for those carefree days of childhood.

Kinsy got her bowl and spoon, taking a chair as far away from anyone else as possible. Thai knew she made a choice to avoid another scene. He took his food and joined her. Cai got up from her seat across the room and sat on Kinsy's other side. Grateful, he didn't know if Cai calculated the move or not, but Kinsy needed a little love and acceptance about now.

After dinner, Cadeo said, "We'll show you to your rooms."

"What about clean up?" Kinsy asked.

"Tonight you are our guests—our very tired guests. Tomorrow will be soon enough to work."

Cai kissed both Thai and Kinsy good night. He found himself longing for the freedom to also kiss Kinsy and wish her sweet dreams. Not only had she been rejected by the children, she had also been rejected by him.

Lan led the ladies to their room, and watching Kinsy walk away pulled at his heart. All those feelings from Yosemite resurfaced. Thai and the boys followed Cadeo to their room. Cadeo passed out oscillating fans to all six of them. "These not only help with the heat, but they also help keep the mosquitoes away."

Each boy claimed one of the six cots, setting their fans on the small tables beside where they'd sleep. Thai grabbed the last one and placed his things on the empty cot near the window.

"Sleep well," Cadeo said on his way out the door. "Tomorrow we'll tour Saigon."

Thai's heart felt as if it dropped all the way to his feet. Perhaps they would tread upon the last place he'd ever seen his mother. A lump rose in his throat.

"Then we'll get busy distributing those Bibles and doing some repair work around here. I'm so glad you came. You have no idea what a blessing you are to Lan and me."

"Good night," they all clamored at once as Cadeo shut the door.

Though he was exhausted, sleep evaded Thai. After a fitful night, the breakfast bell woke him with a start. Thinking about touring Saigon today caused his heart to lodge in his throat. Was he ready to walk her streets again? Truth be known, he didn't think he'd ever be ready. Nonetheless, the heavenly insistence suggested that God was ready. *I can do everything through him who gives me strength.* The verse that Kinsy quoted at Half Dome echoed through his mind. *If she could face her fear of that mountain, I can face Saigon,* he thought with new resolve.

"First, we'll take Ly Thai To Boulevard," Cadeo said as they all loaded into the van. "It's now one of Saigon's major thoroughfares. Then we'll walk in order to get a feel for the life here."

The humidity hung around Thai like a heavy cloak. His

damp clothes clung to his wet skin. On their drive, they passed tons of minuscule eateries. The streets were sometimes cluttered with discarded trash, crowded with people everywhere, and loud with the noises of cars and the drone of voices. He spotted a group of children playing soccer with a tennis ball. They seemed oblivious to the danger of the nearby traffic, just as he and Loi had been.

Once Cadeo parked the van, they strolled by numerous dark, thin women lining the streets, selling various sundries from kiosks and baskets. Every sight, every sound resurrected surreal memories that hurled themselves through Thai like rain pelting a huge jungle leaf during a Vietnamese summer. He seemed suspended between the past and present, not able to fully experience either. An old woman who reminded him of his grandmother peddled sweet rice and proved the catalyst that fully hurled him into the past. Suddenly, he was four again, and his grandmother had just nabbed him by the collar for running through the house. But Thai had only been following Loi.

Finally, his grandmother released him, and Thai joined his brother on the street. In an alley, they stopped to watch a mother and daughter fry dough cakes, wrapping them in dirty newspaper to sell. The past merged with the present, and Thai's stomach rolled at the thought of eating something prepared in such filth. But he pictured himself and Loi doing exactly that, spending the money Mama gave them on street food like banana rice cakes, fried bread, or rice porridge.

The past faded into a distant blur as the poverty overwhelmed Thai. Beggars spotted the street, and one undernourished boy stood out in the crowd. Time no longer existed, and Thai's steps faltered. Familiar-looking eyes stared back at him. *Loi,* his heart screamed but his mind reasoned away the possibility. Tears welled up, rolling freely down his cheeks.

"Thai?" Kinsy spoke from right next to him. She laid her hand on his arm. He grabbed it like a lifeline, squeezing tight.

The little boy moved on through the crowd and Thai decided he must chase him down. He needed to help him! "Wait," Thai called, knowing the child most likely couldn't understand. "I have to find him, Kinsy," he said before sprinting off.

"Thai, wait!" He dismissed her cry. He had to find the boy, and waiting would lessen his chances. Kinsy shouted something else, but her words dropped from his mind in the face of his heart's insistent demands. The boy turned down a dingy alley, and Thai hesitated before following. This alley might very well be the one where the soldier gave him the lighter. His stomach clenched, and his determination to find the boy overruled his aversion. Finally he noticed the child at the alley's opening, begging food from a cart in the next street. The woman turned him away, shaking her head.

Breathless, Thai slowed his pace and neared. The boy looked skeptical, wary. Calling to mind the words from the language tapes, Thai struggle to phrase his sentence in the Vietnamese language. "I want to help you." He reached in his pocket and pulled out all the *dong* he'd brought with him for the day. He wished for the rest of his money hidden in his suitcase at the orphanage.

"For you and your family." He held out the notes.

The young boy looked from the *dong*, to Thai, and back to the money again. Shock registered on his face, then gratitude. He slowly took the notes then bowed. His voice trembled with his thanks as he stuffed the bills in his pocket.

"Take this, too," Thai said, offering him a Vietnamese New Testament.

The boy accepted Thai's gift, turned, and ran. He stopped once, waving a last good-bye before rounding a corner, and he was gone.

Thai pivoted to return to where he'd left the team and bumped into Kinsy. Instinctively, he pulled her into his arms, and they clung to one another, both crying, for the country of their births and its people.

❧

With Thai's arms around her, Kinsy knew they both experienced many of the same emotions. Returning was nothing like she'd expected, much more painful and less joyous than she anticipated. Thai loosened his hold on her. She looked into his watery, red eyes and despised herself for the part she played in causing him to even be on this trip. No wonder he erupted when he learned that she had hidden their trip's destination. Kinsy marveled that he would even speak to her.

"He looked like Loi," Thai explained. He took a deep breath as if hoping to exhale the memory. "He could be me, Kinsy. . .or you. How were we the ones lucky enough to leave, yet unlucky enough to lose everything before we did?"

She only shrugged and shook her head. She had no answers for him, just her own questions.

"This is my country. These are my people. I wanted to forget, but how can I?" He glanced upward, toward the alley walls. "This might even be the very alley where that soldier gave me the lighter that blew up my mother and brother." The tears trickled onto his cheeks, and Kinsy reeled with the force of his words. For once in her life, she didn't push ahead of God or pry for more information.

"How can I help my people? What can I do to make their lives better?"

Her own feelings mirrored Thai's. Her tears flowed again. She cried for the people who shared her ancestry, she cried for this man she'd grown to love more deeply each day, and she cried for herself.

Thai tenderly draped his arm around her and led her back toward the main street. Her vision still hazy from the tears, she leaned against him, letting him guide her. Thai stopped at the place where he'd last seen their team. "I wonder how we'll ever find them?"

"Cadeo said we'd meet at the van at three. He took the kids to eat at one of the approved places on our list and then to do some shopping. I think he sensed we both needed some time to assimilate being back here. I tried to tell you just before you ran, and that's why I came after you. The team had already departed, and I didn't want to be completely alone in this city all afternoon."

He squeezed her shoulders in brief hug. "I'm sorry. Seeing that little boy made me forget everything else. I would have never consciously left you alone here."

"I know," she assured him.

"Suddenly, I'm famished. How about you?"

"Famished and emotionally spent. Sitting down for awhile would be nice."

"There's a café." Thai pointed across the street. "What do you think?"

"It looks safer than most of these street vendors. Let's check our list." Kinsy shuffled through her backpack.

"Yeah, the place is Steve-approved."

Thai took her hand and led her through traffic and into the small, dark building. He held out her chair at a table for two in the corner and took the seat across from her. A young boy came over to take their order. Staring at her, he muttered something in Vietnamese, and quickly left.

Thai's jaw clenched. Kinsy instinctively knew that, considering the boy's glare and derogatory tone, he had said something about her.

"I'm not very hungry after all. Can we leave?" Kinsy stood and hoped to avoid any sort of scene.

An older man approached them. Kinsy bowed. He said something to Thai in Vietnamese while staring at her. Thai's eyes reflected his intent to defend her. She laid a restraining hand on his arm.

"We're leaving." She forced a smile, but more tears burned the back of her eyes. *Thai must think all I do is cry.*

The war Thai fought within battled across his face, but he finally nodded his acceptance of her decision. His pulsating jaw revealed his anger, but he remained outwardly calm, bowing to the man before they left.

Not a word crossed his lips as they strode down the street. He led her to a rusty table, near an alley, and they silently nibbled on a bag of trail mix from Thai's backpack.

"This stuff is a far cry from what we would have eaten. Are you disappointed that I wanted to leave the café?"

He reached across the table and laid his hand on hers. "No, I'm just angry at them for being so rude."

"It doesn't matter, Thai."

"It does to me." He paused as if weighing an important decision. "When I was in junior high, kids who'd been my friends suddenly turned on me because I was different.

They called me yellow-skinned Asian and sometimes even slant-eyes."

"But Vietnamese eyes aren't really slanted."

"I know. But that didn't matter. They chanted, 'Go home where you belong.' When the kid back there called you half-breed, I wanted to deck him, for your sake, for mine, and for every other kid who's ever been picked on."

Touched by his protective attitude, she also experienced a dawning of fresh understanding into his past. Part of his desire for a blond wife had more to do with protection than prejudice. He intended to shelter his future offspring from what he'd been through. A new spark of respect flared within Kinsy.

A stray dog rooting under their table caught her attention. "He's hoping we dropped a scrap of food. Poor, hungry fellow." Thai dropped a handful of the trail mix near his nose.

"Can I bum some *dong* until later? I gave all mine to Loi's look-alike."

Kinsy granted his request.

"I'll be right back," Thai said. He returned with a fairly long bone. "Ox tail for this old bag of bones." Thai gave it to the dog and patted him on the head. "Cadeo said people don't eat dog much anymore."

"Good to hear." She smiled, loving him for spending money on the poor old thing. "I couldn't bring myself to ever even taste dog."

"My grandmother said the same thing. No matter how hungry she was, she'd never cook or eat dog meat." He smiled tenderly. "You would have liked my grandmother. She was a spunky little thing, devoted to the care and feeding of her clan."

"I'm sure I would have. Lan said many women still

dedicate their lives to cooking, cleaning, and meeting the needs of their children, grandchildren, and extended family, especially in the smaller villages."

He nodded. "Have you ever thought about adoption?" Thai's question came out of nowhere.

"Of course I have, since I'm adopted."

"No, I mean about adopting children yourself someday?"

She nodded. "Especially after meeting Cai. I wish I could offer her a family now."

He shot her his heart-melting smile, full of incredulity. "I had the same thought."

eleven

The next day, fear and anticipation rose within Kinsy. The village they pedaled toward, Cau Hai, was the village her mother hailed from. Today her lifelong dream would become reality. On this very day, she would meet some of her extended family. Anh's daughter was coming home.

Between a letter left for her at the orphanage, some facts the McCoys gathered, and an old file Lan possessed, Kinsy knew a few things about her past. Her grandfather, Bay Le, was a chief and respected elder in the remote village. Her father, an American soldier, died protecting the village. Her mother died birthing her. Now Kinsy was pedaling through a foreign land, going home.

The roads were rough and bouncy, but the beautiful terrain made up for the bumpy ride. The foliage was as green as emeralds and jungle-type plants grew in abundance. Kinsy's heart soared. She prayed her grandfather would be one of the Christians in the village expecting the Bibles. Since none of the team were avid bikers, they rode awhile and walked awhile. Everyone pedaled in silence, a bit nervous since each carried a pack full of smuggled Bibles and some Bible tracts with them.

Kinsy knew this moment was orchestrated by God, an answer to her lifetime prayers. As they biked off the beaten path, every fiber of her being balked against the strain. When they stopped for lunch, she'd never experienced such relief at getting off a bike; the seat and her bottom lacked compatibility.

"Only a couple of more miles," Thai said, looking at the map Cadeo drew. After lunch they rested for about half an hour then started on their way. Kinsy barely got a bite of food down. Excitement tied her stomach in knots, making eating next to impossible.

When they arrived at the small village, Thai asked for Nghia Hoa. He followed the directions to a shack with walls made from palm branches and a straw roof. An older Vietnamese gentleman, with thinning white hair, greeted Thai and invited the dozen team members into his home. Weeping when they began unpacking the Bibles, Nghia held each one like a fragile crystal vase. Then Thai helped him carry them to a secret hiding place somewhere out back.

Nghia invited them to sit on straw mats, where he served them sweet smelling banana rice cakes and Coca-Cola to drink. Smiling proudly, he told Thai he'd saved his Coke for special American guests. Thai roughly interpreted what Nghia said, understanding some, but not all.

"Most in this village very poor. American churches send shortwave radios, but most stolen before hear God's word. You work hard to get God's Words into hands and ears of people."

Again Nghia got teary, sorrow etching itself across his lined face. "Bless your faithfulness." He prayed for their group. "Now go. I sell refreshment to travelers as a cover, but none stay long, so neither can you."

Kinsy had Thai ask about her grandfather, Bay Le. Nghia looked concerned, but gave them directions to the Le home. "He's not a friend of God's people," Thai translated the pastor's warning. "Be careful not to expose the underground church or my work to him."

Deeply disappointed by the news, Kinsy desperately desired her grandfather to be a part of the Christian movement here in this village. Kinsy touched the New Testament in her pocket, hoping to present it to the old man as a gift. Now maybe she shouldn't since they'd been seen with Nghia. The team promised him they'd be careful not to put him at risk.

As they walked their bikes towards her grandfather's, Thai asked the team to wait out front. He would accompany Kinsy to the door. He gave her hand a quick squeeze and she whispered, "Pray for me."

"I have been all day," he assured her.

Thai knocked and a young male servant opened the door. Her grandfather lived in a much nicer and larger place than the pastor did.

They bowed low. "May we speak to Bay Le?" Thai asked in his rough Vietnamese.

The servant said, "Mr. Le does not accept visitors."

When Thai translated, Kinsy said, "Tell him I'm his granddaughter, Anh's child."

The servant nodded and closed the door.

"Is he coming back?" Kinsy asked.

"I think so."

Her heart pounded. Meeting her family would not be easy, if even possible. *God, please make a way.* She rubbed her palms against her pant legs.

❧

An uneasiness crept up Thai's spine even before the door opened. A stooped, white haired man glared at Kinsy. His cold eyes sat deep in a wrinkled face. "You liar and fraud," the old man shouted. "I have no daughter, only sons. Do not ever insult my family name again." The old man spit on Kinsy, called her a half-breed, and then slammed his door.

Stunned, Thai removed his outer denim shirt to wipe the spit and tears off her face. He drew her away from the house. "Let's get out of here."

Kinsy stopped halfway to the bikes. An ashen pallor covered her face, blighting out her cheerful demeanor. "Tell me what he said," she whispered.

Thai didn't want to repeat the words, knowing she'd only feel worse, but he knew he must. He repeated the truth as gently as possible.

"Why would he lie?"

"I don't know." Thai knotted his shirt around his waist and led her toward the bikes. "Let's go home."

Kamie hugged Kinsy when they got back to the group. "Are you okay?"

"Not yet," Kinsy said in a raspy whisper, "but I will be."

They climbed on their bikes; nobody said much. *Why, God? Why did you let that happen to her*? Thai asked as they pedaled back toward the orphanage. Immediately, he thought of 2 Corinthians 4:10, *"Through suffering, these bodies of ours constantly share in the death of Jesus so that the life of Jesus may also be seen in our bodies."*

How many times had Thai taught on those verses? As we suffer, we identify more with Christ and become more like him. Even though he desired Kinsy to grow in Christlikeness, he hated for her to hurt. But as humans, hurt was inevitable. Then the truth struck Thai. God allowed his suffering for the exact same reason. Already, Thai was experiencing a certain release from his past. But could he relinquish all his sorrow and let God make him whole?

❧

Heartbroken, Kinsy pedaled on, aching to the very marrow of her bones. A scooter roared past them and stopped. Thai rode up beside the petite woman wearing the pointed hat many of the Vietnamese women wore. He dismounted and the rest of the team stopped a few feet back. Kinsy heard the woman say, "I am Chi, Anh's cousin." Chi's English was coarse but understandable.

Kinsy got off her bike and went to the woman, taking her hands. After being spit on, she wasn't sure she should be so trusting, but this woman appeared to be an ally. "I am Kinsy McCoy. Anh was my mother. She died giving me life."

Chi's eyes shifted. "Anh not dead. Lives in Vung Tau."

Stunned by the woman's fear-filled words, Kinsy said, "No. My mother Anh Le is dead. The note left with me at the orphanage said so."

"Excuse me, Kinsy," Thai interrupted, "we'll be over there under those palms." He pointed toward his destination. "Holler if you need me."

"Will you stay?" She already needed him.

Thai nodded and sent the participants off, but he stayed next to Kinsy.

"I wrote the note. I know what it said." Shame wove itself through Chi's words and across her face.

Kinsy's knees felt like wet noodles. She reached for Thai to steady herself. "What are you saying? I don't understand."

Chi sighed. "My Uncle Bay convinced me it would be best. He is an important Chief in our village. His daughter having child by American soldier embarrassed the family. He disowned her. He did not lie today when he say he have no daughter. As far as he's concerned, he does not."

"How do you know what he said to me?"

"My pastor, Nghia, sent for me and told me your story. Then I went to my Uncle's and his servant disclosed what I had already guessed. Your grandfather—my uncle—rejected you. I am sorry."

Kinsy nodded. "You are a Christian?" She was almost afraid to ask. What if this were some sort of trap?

"Yes, I follow Christ. Only the past few years though, as you must already presume."

"Does my mother follow Christ?" Her biological mother lived somewhere in this country! She was alive!

Pools of sorrow swam in her ebony eyes. "No, she does not."

"My grandfather?" she asked, fairly certain of the answer.

Chi shook her head.

"Did my mother not want me?" Kinsy asked, trying to piece it all together.

"Very much. She love your father. When he was killed, she wanted his child very much. Then your grandfather learned the truth and sent her away. He is powerful man, and he made certain Anh believed you died at birth. He arranged with the doctor for me to take you to the orphanage. I lied and told them your mother died."

Kinsy leaned against Thai, no longer having the strength to stand. "Why?"

"Your grandfather believed she deserved to lose the child because of the shame and disgrace she caused him."

"Does my mother still think I am dead?"

"I told her the truth after I become a follower of Christ. She wept and threw me out. I have not seen her since. But she is only about 120 kilometers from Saigon. Perhaps you can visit. Perhaps you can beg her for my forgiveness."

Kinsy hugged Chi. "I will. I promise. Thank you, Chi. Thank you."

With a furrowed brow, Chi asked "For what do you thank me?"

"For coming after me today and telling me the truth." Kinsy hesitated. "Will my mother want to see me?"

"Very much. She long to see you very much." Chi smiled. "Even though she hates me for what I did, she's happy you live in beautiful, free America."

Chi and Kinsy hugged and cried. Kinsy promised to write her new grandcousin, as they are called here in Vietnam. She took the paper with Chi's address, tucked it in her front pocket, and bid her good-bye. Kinsy watched Chi ride away on her scooter, bouncing along the washboard road.

"I have a mother!" She turned to Thai, knowing there was no one she'd rather share this moment with than him. She loved him with all her heart. She loved him enough to let him go. She loved him enough to wish for all his hopes and dreams to come true, even the ones excluding her from his life forever.

He smiled. "You're amazing." Hugging her close for a brief moment, he then whistled for the kids, motioning for them to join him and Kinsy. Soon they all pedaled toward the orphanage. Kinsy nearly floated, no longer dwelling on her sore leg muscles. "My birth mother is alive!" she repeated on the ride home.

❧

In the evening after dinner and cleanup, Kinsy joined Thai out on the porch. Just seeing her, having her near brought him pleasure. The rest of the team read stories to the kids and helped tuck them into bed while he and Kinsy gazed at the star-filled, inky sky.

"Feels good to get our first set of Bibles delivered," Thai commented.

"Sure does," she agreed.

A breeze played with her hair and he wished for the freedom to do the same. During their trip, the chains of Thai's past seemed to be dropping away from his soul, link by link. Yet, a haunted little boy was still locked away in the recesses of his heart.

"And I have hope for my grandfather to someday find Christ, since there is an active, growing church right within his village."

"And both you and Chi will be praying," Thai said. "I'll pray, too." He paused before adding, "I spoke to Cadeo and requested the next two days off and the use of the van. He gave his blessing for me to drive you to Vung Tau. He'll keep the rest of the team busy with chores around here. I even called your dad and made sure we got his blessing. I hope you don't mind."

Grateful, almond-shaped eyes gazed into his. She smiled slightly. "I don't mind at all."

twelve

Midmorning rain pelted the van. Drops beat on the green leaves of the surrounding jungle plants. Water gushed from a gray sky and reduced the road to a series of endless brown puddles.

Kinsy remained silent as Thai concentrated on the slick, wet road. On Highway 1, a concrete divider kept the chaos going in the same direction. Thai turned onto a smaller road heading out toward the coast. Shanties lined the road. The terrain was flat. Rice paddies, swampy and green, and fruit groves filled the land on either side of them. The mountains stood regally, far off on the horizon behind them.

Kinsy wondered how different her life might have been had her Vietnamese grandfather not interfered. She wouldn't be a McCoy, or have ever met Thai. She might not have even ever met Christ. Kinsy clung to God's sovereignty, knowing he knew from the beginning of time how her life would turn out.

They passed a strip of settlements. "Fisher folks' homes," Thai said. The huts built with grass roofs sat on stilts raising them high off the water below. Driving by a tiny, grandmotherly woman with wrinkled hands and face, Kinsy wondered what her own Grandmother Le might look like. She thought back to the grandfather she met just yesterday and prayed for him again.

They rolled past some ancient buildings with paint peeling off in large chunks. Windows were thrown open wide, probably in hopes of catching a cool breeze off the sea. Children. Everywhere children ran and played.

"That was my life," Thai said, nostalgia filling his voice. "Loi and I ran freely through the village streets with our cousins." The ache in the words pierced her heart.

Thai followed Chi's directions to the home of Anh Le—the home of Kinsy's mother. The small beach cottage sat apart from the large front house. After parking the van, they walked side by side to door. He touched her arm briefly as if to say, *I'm here if you need me*, and she squeezed his hand in appreciation. Her stomach knotted, her hands trembled, and her pulse accelerated. A film of sweat dampened her palms.

Thai knocked on the door. Sucking in a deep breath, Kinsy held it. A woman with dyed red hair and excessive makeup answered their knock. Kinsy's heart dropped in disappointment. This wasn't the motherly image she expected.

"We're looking for Anh Le," Thai said in English.

"Who wants her?" the woman asked in near flawless English.

"I do. I have come from America to visit her," Kinsy answered.

The woman's face softened, but she didn't let her guard down completely. "Why would you come so far to visit Anh Le?"

Kinsy knew this was her mother. She'd seen the hope flash in her eyes when she'd mentioned America. She bit her bottom lip, afraid to say the words. She took a deep breath. "I am her daughter, Kinsy McCoy."

The woman's eyes filled with tears and she leaned against the door jam. She tenderly looked at Kinsy and tears ran freely down both of their faces. Kinsy reached to the woman, and she clung to her.

"I am Anh—your mother," she whispered in a broken voice.

Kinsy moved toward her, pulling her tiny mother into her arms. She had no idea how long they stood there, hugging, crying, and laughing. Her mother pulled back, taking her hand. "Please come in."

Kinsy looked back at Thai. His eyes glistened with tears as well, and she knew he must be longing for his own mother. "This is my *ban,* Thai. This is my mother," Kinsy said with pride, "Anh Le."

"Welcome, Kinsy's friend. It is my pleasure to have you both in my home."

The cottage perched on the edge of a cliff over the beach. Her mother led them out onto the balcony jutting out over the water. Waves lapped against the rock embankment a few feet below. Two coconut palms shaded the side of the house.

"It's beautiful here," Kinsy whispered.

"It's my sanctuary." Her mother turned away from the sea and faced her visitors. "I have soda. May I offer you one?"

Kinsy and Thai answered simultaneously, "Yes, please," and followed Anh back into her home.

Her mother's house was decorated tastefully, much more American than the others she'd seen. When her mother returned with the sodas, she and Kinsy sat together on the sofa. Thai took a nearby chair.

"I used to own the whole estate, but the Communists seized everything. I was only able to buy back this little studio, a fraction of what I once had." Kinsy wondered what her mother did to obtain such wealth. "How did you find me?" Anh asked.

Kinsy told her about coming to this country on a humanitarian aid trip and meeting Chi. She chose not to mention her grandfather, the way he treated her, or his denying having a daughter. If her mother asked about him, Kinsy would be honest, but why cause more hard feelings between them if she didn't have to?

"Chi sends her love and continues to beg for your forgiveness," Kinsy said.

"Let's not talk about our unhappy pasts, or our wretched, deceitful relations. Tell me all about you, your life from as far back as you can remember. Come talk to me while I prepare lunch for us."

Kinsy followed her mother into the corner kitchen area. Thai excused himself and went out on the balcony. Kinsy leaned against the counter dividing the tiny cooking area from the main room.

"Thoughtful, considerate, and handsome young man," her mother said when Thai left. Kinsy decided not to answer. Instead, she gave her mother a brief, thirty-minute overview of her adoptive family and her life in the states. Anh got teary a few times.

"I'm so glad you live in beautiful, free America with a good family and a happy life." She hugged Kinsy. "Lunch is ready. Go fetch your young man."

As Kinsy stepped toward the balcony, the words *your young man* clenched her heart. She thought back to their kiss at Yosemite and wondered if she would ever feel his lips against hers again. Thai napped in the sun on a lounge chair. His tranquil expression tugged at her heart. She sat on the edge of the chaise and longed to trace the outline of his cheek.

Thai's eyes opened; their tenderness stole her breath. Smiling, he asked, "So what do you think of your mom?"

"She seems wonderful." *Just like you.* "Lunch is ready."

When they were all seated at the table, Anh served them

steamed rice cakes filled with pepper pork and sweet beans. Kinsy liked the spicy food very much. Anh asked Thai about his background and how he ended up in the US. Giving a brief overview, he didn't expound on anything Kinsy didn't already know. She wondered about what happened between the time the soldier gave him the lighter and his mother and brother were killed. But once more, Kinsy covered her curiosity.

❧

Anh Le reminded Thai of his mother and his responsibility for her death. She didn't look or act like her, yet they were both petite Vietnamese women who loved their children. Bile rose up Thai's throat, and he thought he would choke. If only he had hidden the lighter from Loi, perhaps his mother and Loi wouldn't have been killed. Thai might himself have died, but anything would be better than knowing he was in any way connected to his mother's and Loi's death.

"Tell me about you now," Kinsy pleaded. "Tell me about my father."

Anh's eyes misted over. "Your father. . ." Affection satiated her face and her voice. She dreamily stared past Kinsy as if she were ensnared by another realm, a time she could never relive and only visit in her memories. "Your father was Sergeant Major William Harlow, United States Marines. His dark hair and sparkling green eyes made him the most handsome man I'd ever met."

Anh rose and went to a small chest sitting on a dresser. Removing several pictures, she handed them to Kinsy. Kinsy studied each picture, running her fingers over the faces as if touching them made them more real. She bit her lips in an attempt to stop the threatening tears.

"He was handsome and you were very beautiful. Is the

baby in this picture me?"

Anh nodded. "Chi gave me the picture when she confessed her wrongdoing."

After several more minutes of staring at the pictures, Kinsy passed all but one of them to Thai. She continued to stare at it.

He looked at the beautiful Asian baby—Kinsy—and imagined what her children would look like. An unexpected longing for children of his own with dark hair and eyes filled Thai. He would give to them something Thai never knew: the security of his approval.

Thai had been loved, but not secure. His adopted dad was a military man and didn't have much tolerance for teary-eyed boys. "Take it like a man," was his motto. Thai's cautious and sensitive nature got on his nerves. Instead of grieving for his mother and Loi, he tried to bury all the pain and fear because he didn't intend to upset his new dad.

All the grief from all those years suddenly bubbled up, and he could no longer contain his emotions. Abruptly, he rose from the table. "I think I'll take a walk."

❧

Kinsy knew Thai wrestled with his own demons from the past. She ached for him. At least part of her past could be resolved. His never could because everyone had died. She said a quick prayer for him.

"Let me help you clear these while you tell me about your life." Kinsy rose and started carrying dishes to the sink.

Anh started farther back than Kinsy had expected. "My parents married without the blessing of either family. I hoped because they did, they'd understand my love for Bill was as intense and real as theirs had been. However they neither understood it or accept our relationship." She paused and swallowed hard.

Kinsy filled the sink with soapy water and started to wash. Her mother, while rinsing and drying, continued her story.

"My father told us they lived on rice and love under a leaky roof in a one room shack. Moving to a little village to escape the hostility of their families, my father was eventually elected a chieftain and became an important man. I think somewhere along the way he forget his humble roots and their passionate beginning. Anyway, I was born first, followed by seven brothers."

"Eight children. Quite a clan." And Kinsy was a part of the clan, tied by blood. She handed her mother another plate.

"It's not unusual for Vietnamese families to have lots of children, especially in those days. My parents, they worked hard, scraped by, and saved, proving to their families they'd made something of themselves."

"Did they ever make peace with either set of your grandparents?" Kinsy washed the last pan.

"Sadly, no. In Vietnam one must always respect and honor one's parents. Even at forty or fifty years of age, a person must never disagree with their elders. It is expected of us to bow, nod, and obey. A marriage without blessing is the same as a death. My parents died to their families when they chose to wed."

"How tragic," Kinsy said, saddened by all the division in her newfound family. She wiped down the counters and stove with her wet dishrag.

"I did meet my grandparents. By my own father disowning me, they accepted me. Funny how that works. They are all dead now though, but I got to know them a little." Anh stood on tiptoe to slide the plates into their rightful place.

"Did you ever fall in love again or marry?" Kinsy asked

when they settled back on the sofa.

Anh shook her head. "I am a prostitute, Kinsy." She held her head high, raising her chin as if to say, I am not ashamed of it either.

Kinsy's heart dropped, as did her mouth. Her weak, quiet, "Oh," said more than a thousand words might have.

Her mother rose and walked to the balcony door. She faced Kinsy. "When I lost Bill, my family, and then you, nothing mattered. All love and happiness had been stripped from me. I didn't desire to love again because I didn't want to feel that much pain again—not ever. Rather than risking heartache again, I chose a life of distance and wealth. And I'm sure somewhere inside me I intended to hurt my father as much as he'd hurt me. Having a prostitute for a daughter brings much shame upon the family. Now, it's nothing more than a way of life—and my livelihood."

She paused, looking out to sea. Kinsy noticed Thai leaning against the front door. His face reflected the same surprise and sorrow she wrestled with.

Anh continued her story without turning around. "Men don't fall in love with prostitutes. They only use them for their pleasure and pay them well. In no time, I'd amassed a small fortune and bought this lovely estate. After the American soldiers left, I rebuilt my clientele with wealthy businessmen. I lost it all in 1975 to the communist regime. As I told you before I'd saved enough cash to buy this little beach house back."

She turned back to Kinsy. "Now will you disown me too?"

Kinsy went to her, taking her hands. "You are my birth mother. We share a tie stronger than your career choice." Her vision blurred. "I feel sad you've spent such a long time without knowing or being loved. Money may buy you beautiful things, but it doesn't buy happiness. And things don't fill a lonely heart."

Anh stroked Kinsy's hair. "You are much too wise for your young age, my beautiful daughter." She returned to the sofa. "You are right. I'm a lonely middle-aged woman with no love in my heart or life, at least not until today." Her words and smile warmed Kinsy.

❧

"Thai, welcome back," Anh said. "Why don't we stroll down the beach, so you two can see more of my little tourist town? Designed with the foreign oil workers and executives in mind, it beckons all to relax and enjoy life," she said in a singsong voice as if she were reading a brochure.

Her clientele, Thai thought. "I'd love a walk, and the beach just happens to be your daughter's favorite place in the world."

Anh sent Kinsy a warm look. "Mine, too." She reached for Kinsy's hand. "I'd like to hear more about both of you. I've talked much too much already," Anh said, leading them out the door.

"And I still want to hear more about you and my father," Kinsy added.

The three of them strolled down the beach toward the tourist area. Kinsy carried her sandals, and he remembered her doing the same thing in L.A. Then she waded through the lapping waves. Since arriving in Vietnam everything she did intrigued and impressed him, and Thai wondered if he was truly falling in love for the first time in his life.

They walked in silence, enjoying the afternoon, the beauty surrounding them, and digesting all that had transpired today. When they hit the tourist beach, a mob of vendors descended on them, pulling at their sleeves and pushing bowls of clams and snails into their hands. Teenage girls shoved warm cans of soda, baskets of fruit, and bottles of water at them. Sellers outnumbered prospective buyers about five to one.

All three shook their heads vigorously. Finally the vendors left and found new prey. "Most of the tourists are Russian businessmen. Many are part of the Russian oil interest headquartered in our little resort town," Anh said.

Thai noticed that several men recognized Kinsy's mother. The way they looked at her made him sick. They didn't see Anh as a human with feelings, only entertainment for themselves. One younger man eyed Kinsy. Thai grabbed her hand, letting the fellow know she wasn't on the market.

Kinsy smiled up at him. Her hand rested in his, her skin velvet soft. Anh rented sun chaises and they settled on them.

"Here in Vietnam, most take an afternoon nap." Anh yawned and closed her eyes. "Americans don't have time for such frivolity, do they?"

"Not often," Thai said. "We're much too busy to enjoy life."

"How is that saying? Something about Rome?"

Thai and Kinsy laughed. "When in Vietnam," they both said, "do as the Vietnamese."

"That is the one." Anh smiled. "Join me in a nap, and then I'll tell you about your father and me."

"You've got yourself a deal," Kinsy agreed, closing her eyes.

thirteen

Kinsy woke up first. Her mother and Thai both still slept. She padded along the water's edge. So much had occurred in the last few days she was on emotional overload. She'd need months to process it all.

Noticing Thai and her mother awake and talking, she returned to her chaise.

"Tell me about your orphanage experience, Thai," Anh requested.

"After my mother's death, everything is a blur." Thai looked away from Kinsy and Anh, staring out across the water. "After I lost my family, an American soldier took me to an American-run orphanage that was overcrowded. I slept on the floor with one blanket."

"Kinsy, do you remember anything about your orphanage experience?" her mother asked.

"No. I was adopted before I turned a year old." Kinsy gazed at Thai, thirsting for every detail he provided. However, she knew from the few bits of past he had already shared that he was glossing over many gut-wrenching details.

"My adoptive family said, as near as they could tell, I was there about six months. Shortly before Saigon fell, they herded us like little animals onto a cargo plane and flew us to the U.S. It was another nine months or so before my adoption."

"Was Tong there too?" Kinsy muttered.

"He slept next to me on the cold, hard floor, and we ended up on the same plane. When he cried at night, I tried to comfort him the way I remembered my Mama did for me. We almost got separated and sent to different orphanages, but someone recognized the bond we shared and kept us together. At that point, I think we became a package deal."

"So the Leopolds adopted you together," Anh asked.

Thai nodded. "Tong adjusted better to life with our new family than I did. I closed myself off from them, not wanting to take a chance on loving more people who might die. For some reason in my little boy mind, it was only safe to love Tong."

Thai sighed and looked back at Anh. "Anyway, about all I remember about the orphanage is Tong, a cold hard floor, and then the plane ride. Not much else."

Kinsy longed to comfort him, but what could she possibly say or do to help? Instead she stared out over the water, her heart aching for the little boy who'd lost too much.

"Say, it's almost time for dinner." Anh switched the subject. "Shall we walk to a little café I know?"

Kinsy and Thai stood up and both stretched. "Now it's your turn, Anh. Tell us how you met Kinsy's father."

The three walked side by side with Anh in the middle. "The village of Cau Hai, where I grew up, had a dozen American marines assigned to protect it. Your father was one of the dirty dozen, as they liked to call themselves. Their mission, Bill told me, was the protection of village elders and chiefs and politicians favorable to the democratic regime in the South."

She turned down another street. "This way. Anyhow, Bill was stationed in our village for almost three years.

The first year, my seventeenth, he stayed to himself and just befriended other soldiers. We had no contact, except I and about every other girl in the village thought he had the dreamiest eyes we'd ever seen. We'd watch him from our windows. He was by far the best looking Marine to come our way."

She stopped in front of a small café. "Here we are."

Thai held the door. Smells from America, steak and hamburger, increased Kinsy's hunger. Both Kinsy and Anh stepped inside. Once they were seated, Anh requested English menus.

"I've decided on a good old juicy T-bone. No rice, vegetables, or soup for this boy." Thai closed his menu.

"I think I'll follow Thai's lead," Anh said.

"Might as well." Kinsy laid her menu on the pile.

After their orders were taken, Kinsy asked, "What happened the next year?"

"Because the Viet Cong raided our village at night taking our young males as *volunteers* and stole our food and other supplies, the Marines started night missions to ambush the V.C. It helped for a while until they figured out the game plan. During one week near the end of Bill's first year, ten out of the twelve Marines were killed. Bill said over those next couple of years the squad never reached full strength again, and over the next six months, thirty-six Americans died defending our village."

A tear slid down her cheek, followed by another, then another. Kinsy thought of each life represented by those tears, men protecting her grandfather and the other important men from this small village. Anh blotted the glistening moisture from her cheeks with her napkin. "Most of the villagers appreciated the Americans, but a few had the nerve to complain. How can you complain about someone giving their life for you?"

Thai's eyes met Kinsy's. She saw the same spark in them she experienced. A window of opportunity presented itself for them to share Christ. "Have you ever heard of Jesus?" Thai asked.

Anh looked suspicious. "Chi mentioned Him. I am not interested."

"But He gave His life for you," Kinsy interjected. "What you said about the American soldiers made me think of Jesus. He did the same thing. He died in our place." Kinsy pulled a thin Bible from her pocket and held it out to her. "Will you at least read the book of John?"

She shook her head. "I cannot read English."

"This Bible is written in Vietnamese," Kinsy said.

Her mother tentatively reached for the book Kinsy offered. "I will think about it. No promises though."

"Agreed." Kinsy nodded her head. *Father, please open her eyes to the truth. May she see her need for a Savior. Open her heart to You, Lord.* "So when did you and my father become friends?" Kinsy changed the subject, careful not to push her mother away.

"Just after those ten men died. I was angry with my own father because he didn't like the boy I was seeing and forbade me to see him again. I'd taken a walk to cool off. Near the edge of the village in a thick grove of trees, I heard wailing. Thinking someone was hurt, I ran and found your father sitting on a fallen log, head in his hands, crying like a baby.

"I approached him slowly, fearing he'd been shot. Kneeling before him, I gently touched his arm, and asked if he was hurt. He shook his head. Uncertain what to do, I rose to leave. In a broken voice and hard to understand Vietnamese, he said don't go. He patted the log next to him, so I sat beside him while he wept. Soon I was weeping too.

"At that moment, our hearts and lives bonded irrevocably, though nothing happened between us for many months. We met each afternoon on our log. I helped him improve his Vietnamese, and he taught me English. Ah, our dinner is here." She seemed relieved to get a break from the painful story.

They all ooed and ahhed over the steak. "Good choice, Thai," Anh said. "Now tell me how you two met."

Thai and Kinsy took turns sharing their story, both making certain to leave out the romantic parts, just as Thai had left out so much about his past. After dinner they walked back to the beach house. While Thai unloaded their things from the van, she and Anh stepped out onto the balcony. The water reflected the moonbeams as they danced along the rippling waves like fairies sprinkled in gold dust.

"I'm so glad you're spending the night. Two days isn't long to catch up on a lifetime, is it?" Anh asked. The breeze lifted tuffs of her red hair and feathered it around her cheeks.

Kinsy reached for her hand. "No, but we can write and call each other."

Her mother kissed her cheek. "I'm glad you came."

Kinsy smiled. "Me, too." She yearned to hear the rest of the story about her father, but stopped herself from pushing too much. For the first time, Kinsy was finding herself content to wait for God to naturally unfold the events of her life.

Later, Kinsy found her things in a room, decorated in

white eyelet. Feminine and beautiful, the room made her feel like a princess. After a shower, she lay in the middle of the big four poster bed, swallowed up by a soft feather mattress. She was sure she fell asleep with a smile on her face.

❧

Thai, too tense to sleep, stepped out onto the balcony. The cool night air somewhat refreshed his battered emotions. The ocean beat against the rocks below, reminding him of God's awesome power. His soul was still hollow in the aftermath of the afternoon release of his solitary grief. He stood still, breathing in the salty air. The rhythmical waves felt as if they bathed his soul in a sweet, healing salve. When he rushed out of the house after holding Kinsy's baby picture, Thai had been overcome with a grief more potent than any he had allowed himself to experience. He blindly dashed along the village streets until he once again found himself in an alley. Out of the pedestrians' sight, Thai collapsed against the dingy wall and slid to the ground while sobs erupted from him. For the first time, he opened the door of that dark room in his soul and allowed the four-year-old within to release all his agony. He no longer lay face-first in the dirt of the orphanage driveway. Instead, he stood up, stepped forward, and began reaching out to embrace the future God had planned for him.

"You love her, don't you?" He hadn't realized Anh was out there with him, until she spoke from the swing.

Thai startled and turned. "I beg your pardon?"

She rose and came to stand next to him at the railing. "Kinsy. You're in love with her."

Thai sighed and gripped the handrail.

"It's written all over your face every time you look at her. I recognize that look," she whispered. "Bill once gazed at me with those same starry eyes."

A kindred spirit, fierce and unrelenting, bound them in new respect. They'd both loved and lost to the Vietnam conflict. Almost three decades later, the pain still lingered for each of them.

"I think I do love her," he said, in awe of his own admission. "I've been really struggling with a lot of stuff." He stared at the full moon. "The last seventeen years—since I was about thirteen—I've been determined to forget my Asian heritage. I promised myself I'd do what my brother has done—marry a blond, have blond children, and live the American dream."

"Then Kinsy came along. . ."

Thai nodded. "Kinsy and Cai."

"Cai?" she sounded defensive.

Thai chuckled. "Don't worry, she's not another woman. She's a little girl we met at the orphanage. I just keep having this vision of the three of us building a life together, but I've been against the idea of having an Asian wife."

"Are you prejudiced against your own people?" She sounded disappointed.

"No. At least not the way you mean. I'm responsible for my mother's and brother's deaths." He told her the whole ugly story, the one only he and Tong knew. Never taking his eyes off the moon, he avoided the disgust he knew must be present in Anh's eyes.

"It's been hard to look into Kinsy's eyes without seeing my mother and beating myself up all over again for taking that lighter." Tears as hot as his self-incrimination trickled down his cheeks and plopped on the balcony railing like minuscule pools of pain.

Anh wrapped her arm around him with a gentle maternal

touch. "You were four years old, Thai. The Viet Cong fooled men much older and wiser than you. Many adults fell for the same trick. You were not responsible. Do you hear what I am saying?"

Thai finally looked at her.

"Maybe this God you believe in spared you for a reason."

Never having considered that, Thai had only believed he should have been the one to die, not his mother, not Loi. After all, he'd been the foolhardy one.

"How old is Cai?"

"Four-and-a-half."

"What if the same scenario happened with her, and an older child took the lighter, blowing up the orphanage. Would you blame Cai or the one who gave her the lighter?"

Worded like that it sounded ridiculous.

"The one who gave her the lighter would be responsible. Thai, the V.C. killed your mother, not you. You were only a victim of the war. You must forgive yourself and go on."

Her words poured over him like a soothing balm and intensified the healing he knew the Lord had begun to complete that very afternoon. She was right. He was a victim, not a perpetrator. He took her hand, holding it tightly. "Thank you, Anh," he whispered. "I think I was on the verge of realizing all of that, but you just helped me take the final step in dealing with my past."

"You're welcome, and call me Mom. I'm sure one day soon we'll be related." She winked.

❧

Kinsy awoke early to the tapping of a woodpecker. Pale golden light streamed through the eyelet curtains. Rolling over, she buried her head under a pillow. Groggy and annoyed by the intruder, she emerged from her cozy cocoon. Maybe if she threw rocks, the bird would find someone else to aggravate.

She put on her pink terry cloth robe, fumbled for her slippers, and finally arrived at the balcony. "Good morning." Her mother's voice greeted her cheerfully from the porch swing.

"Is it?" Kinsy asked. "I came to kill a woodpecker or two."

"Those aren't woodpeckers. They are women searching for clams."

"What?"

She pointed out over the edge of the balcony. "Go look for yourself."

Kinsy moved to the railing and noticed the beach was much wider this morning than last night. Several women climbed over the newly exposed rocks and chipped clams loose with miniature sickle-like picks. Their wide pointed hats hid their faces in the shadow of the brim.

"Would you like some tea?"

Kinsy nodded and plopped defeated onto the swing next to her mother. "I guess I won't throw rocks at the ladies. They probably wouldn't appreciate that."

Her mother laughed and poured her a cup of tea from the service sitting next to her. "Your father hated being awakened too," she said, a reminiscent twist to her mouth.

"Oh?" Kinsy asked. Reaching for the tea, she held her breath, hoping that her mother would continue the story of her first and only love.

Anh nodded and dreamily gazed past her daughter. "Yes, we became the best of friends. We shared everything. Our first day together on the log, Bill told me he no longer intended to befriend any of the men who were in his unit. A man who had come the day before died within twelve hours, and Bill couldn't stand to lose any more friends. He said he only needed and wanted one friend—me. Instead of learning about the men, he intended to learn about me, embrace our culture, learn our language, and study our history. He asked me to be his teacher and friend. I said yes and cherished the honor."

She smiled as yesteryear's tale continued to unfold. "Those were the most treasured months of my life. We met on our log each day. He absorbed all I taught him like a thirsty sponge. Then he began to teach me about life and love.

"One day during an English lesson, he said the word kiss and pointed to his mouth. I frowned, not understanding what he meant. Asking if he meant lips, he shook his head no. Tongue? I stuck mine out, but again, he shook his head. A devilish grin settled on his handsome face, and he asked if I wished for him to show me a kiss."

Her voice broke, but her face glowed with the happiness of a tender memory. "I nodded and he taught me to kiss. This was the summer of my eighteenth year, but I'd never been kissed before. Still, I feel like he's the only man I ever kissed. Plenty have kissed me, but I have never really kissed the way I kissed him."

With a pleading look in her eyes, she gazed at Kinsy. "Please do not think your father and I shared a cheap affair. He loved me deeply as I loved him and asked my father for my hand in marriage, but it was denied. My father slapped me around and forbade me to see him again. But it was too late. I loved him too deeply.

"We said our wedding vows to one another. The old log where we met was our witness." Eyes filled with tenderness held Kinsy's rapt attention. "Then I gave myself to him as a wife gives herself to her husband. He only had a year left in the Marines, and planned to send for me. Ten months later, just two months before he was to ship home, he was killed in an ambush."

No longer able to hold her tears at bay, Kinsy cried for the father she never knew and for the mother who'd lost so much. She hugged her mom close.

"When you find a man who loves you that much, Kinsy, don't ever let him go. A woman is lucky to be cherished once in a lifetime."

"My other dad says every woman deserves to be cherished. Her value is far above rubies. Is that why you never looked for another love?"

Nodding, she said, "There could be no other love to compare. It would not be fair to expect another man to live up to Bill. He was my once in a lifetime dream come true, and he will live in my heart forever." She walked to the balcony railing. "He believed in your Jesus Christ."

Like rain in a thunderstorm, tears of joy poured forth. Her birth father resided in heaven, and some day they would meet. One day, they would worship God together. "Mother—"

She spun toward Kinsy, a smile lighting her teary face. "That is the first time you called me Mother. Thank you. You have no idea what a gift hearing you say the word is."

"You are my mother—my beloved mother." Kinsy rose and went to her, holding her hands. "You can see Bill again. If he believed in Jesus Christ, the Son of God, he is in heaven for eternity. You can join him there someday—if only you will believe."

A tiny flicker of interest danced in her mother's eyes.

"Mother, please read the book of John. You'll get a clear picture of who Jesus is and why He came. John says, 'Yet to all who receive Him—Jesus Christ—to all who believe in His name, He gives them the right to become children of God.' My father will be in heaven, and so will I. Please be there, too." Kinsy stopped herself from begging on her hands and knees.

"I will read John," Anh agreed.

Thai came through the sliding glass door carrying a tray laden with omelets, fruit, and toast. "I thought you ladies might be hungry."

"Starved," they both said at once.

They spent the rest of the morning relaxing and sharing funny childhood memories. After lunch, Thai loaded their things. Kinsy promised to visit her mother twice a week for the next three weeks.

Anh hugged both Kinsy and Thai in a bear hug. She wept as they drove away.

fourteen

Three weeks passed before Thai worked up his nerve and found the right moment to ask Kinsy to marry him. She gone to see her mother several times, and yesterday he'd gone along. When they'd found a few moments alone, Thai promised Anh he would propose before they left Vietnam tomorrow morning. He'd put the proposal off in case Kinsy said no. Though her mother assured him Kinsy was his for the asking, his confidence lagged. Sometimes he'd catch glimpses of tenderness in her eyes, but mostly she was guarded in his presence. Thai only knew that he loved her and that his love had been growing since their trek up Half Dome. If she planned to be cherished, he was the man.

Her mother had been reading from John everyday. She asked a lot of challenging questions. She had Thai and Kinsy digging to find answers. Kinsy even e-mailed her dad for help. Kinsy and Thai both felt confident Anh would some day give her heart to Christ.

The sun neared the western horizon, stretching golden fingers across the azure sky. Thai and Kinsy meandered along the Saigon River with Cai between them, holding each of their hands. His heart warmed, thinking of the picture-perfect family they resembled.

"Swing me," Cai pleaded.

They each held one of Cai's arms and gently swayed her back and forth.

"Butterfly," Cai squealed. That was their signal that she wanted down to go chase the poor, unsuspecting insect.

Thai whispered a prayer as Cai skipped off after her prey. He took a deep breath. God was handing him the opportunity he'd prayed for. Swallowing hard, Thai hoped to dislodge his stomach which had somehow crawled up his throat.

He stopped walking and so did Kinsy. They stood together watching their tiny charge running through the tall grass after the elusive creature fluttering over her head.

"I love her." Kinsy's quiet words echoed his thoughts. "Don't you wish we could take her back with us?"

"More than just about anything." Being Cai's daddy ranked second on his list of desires right under being Kinsy's husband. "And I think you've just come up with the best idea I've ever heard. We could get married and come back to take her home with us."

Her eyes rounded and her mouth fell open. "I didn't mean that the way you took it, Thai."

"So what." He bowed down on one knee. "Marry me, Kinsy. I—"

"I can't." Pleasure didn't light her face, as he'd hoped. Mortification or maybe even horror more aptly described the emotions flashing from her eyes.

"But. . ." Before he could finish, she bolted toward the orphanage without a backward glance.

Thai rose and brushed the mud off his jeans. His throat burned as he reeled with the confusion over what went wrong. So much for Anh and her certainty about Kinsy returning his love.

Thai held Cai's hand and they walked back toward the orphanage. Would she be better off here or in a single parent family with only a dad? If she were a boy, Thai would press forward with confidence, but he knew a little girl needed a mom.

❧

Kinsy darted away from Thai, wishing she could run away from her mouth as well. She did it again! Just when she thought she'd learned to let God be God and wait on Him, she'd thrown herself at Thai, forcing a proposal from his lips. *Why? Why, can't I ever learn*? she lambasted herself, not sure she'd ever been so disgusted. *First, I forced him to come to Vietnam, then I used emotional blackmail, implying that if he'd marry me, we could adopt Cai and take her home with us.*

The grass whispered beneath her feet as she rushed ahead. When the orphanage wasn't much farther, Kinsy slowed to a walk, holding her aching side and attempting to slow her breathing. *How foolish to imply Thai had to saddle himself with me to adopt Cai. Single people adopt all the time.* Her face burned with embarrassment. Thai was obviously still dealing with his past and Kinsy wasn't certain he knew how he felt about himself—much less her. Even for Cai, someday Kinsy would regret forcing Thai's hand in marriage. *Lord, I'm so sorry. Please forgive me for once again running ahead of Your timing, pushing people to get what I want. I thought I was learning. But I still have far to go.* Looked as if Kinsy would be apologizing to poor Thai, again.

❧

The next morning, Thai chewed the last bite of his *banh cuon,* a treat that tasted similar to pigs-in-a-blanket. The rice crepes with sausage had been one of his favorite breakfasts as a boy. The team now had two hours to play with the children and say their good-byes. All their belongings were already loaded in the van.

Yesterday, Kinsy avoided Thai until the going away party. When Thai finally worked up the nerve to approach her at the end of the party, Kinsy muttered a terse apology and confined herself to her room for the rest of the evening. Feeling as if the whole mission team and Cadeo and Lan were watching his and Kinsy's every move, Thai had glanced over his shoulder, only to have his suspicions confirmed. The group at least had the decency to continue in their idle chatter while Thai slipped outside for some time alone.

This morning, Kinsy had risen early to help Lan with breakfast, and Thai had been busy loading their luggage. Regret filled her eyes every time they met his, but with the bustle of their final hours in Nam, they might not get to talk until the plane ride home.

The team passed out the balloons and hard candy they'd purchased for the orphans. Cai asked Thai to read her a book. When they finished, she ran off to see Miss Kinsy. He played soccer with a group of boys in the front of the orphanage.

"There you are, Thai," Cadeo said. "It's time." He tapped his watch with his index finger.

Thai found Kinsy in a rocker with Cai. "We need to round everyone up," he said quietly, hating to disrupt the tender scene.

Kinsy nodded, attempting to ease Cai off her lap, but Cai wrapped her arms around Kinsy's neck. "Please don't leave me here." Cai started crying.

"Honey, we've talked about this." Kinsy lovingly held Cai close.

"We have to go home." Kinsy's eyes filled with tears.

Thai knelt in front of the rocker. Tears filling his eyes as well. "Cai, we'll write to you," he promised.

Her sobs turned to wails, and his heart felt like someone ran it through a meat grinder. Thai helped Kinsy pry her loose, only to have her latch onto him; her death grip around his neck made breathing and speaking difficult. "I'll carry you while I round up the kids, but then you have to be a brave girl and say good-bye." He sent a helpless look Kinsy's direction, but she only shrugged.

Cai nodded her agreement and her howls quieted to snivels. Thai gathered the team together, they all said their good-byes, and gave many hugs on their way to the van.

When everyone was settled in the van, Thai tried to put Cai down, but her arms held his neck for dear life. "Take me with you," she begged. "Be my daddy."

Her words clenched his heart. "I can't. I want to, but I can't."

How do you explain the need for a mother to a four year old? He swallowed hard, hoping to dislodge the lump embedded in his throat.

"Cai, you must let Mr. Thai leave. He has an airplane to catch."

Lan sought to reason with her, but Cai only turned her face away and buried her nose in Thai's shoulder. Lan pried Cai's arms from around his neck. Finally free, he climbed into the passenger seat of the van, unable to tear his gaze from Cai.

She screamed, reaching for him. "Don't leave me! Please my daddy. Don't leave me." She reminded him of that inconsolable, heartbroken little boy who'd just witnessed the demise of his mother and brother. His heart hurt so much he could scarcely breathe.

Surely, one Dad was better than no family at all.

"Wait," Thai said, just as Cadeo shifted into first. He unbuckled his seatbelt. Tears dripped off his chin onto his shirt. He no longer cared who saw him cry. He didn't try to hide the fact that it was killing him to leave Cai behind. He reached for her and she leapt into his waiting arms.

Carrying her to the porch steps, he sat down. "I love you, Cai. I want to be your daddy." The words came out muffled and raspy. "I'll be back for you, I promise. Will you wait for me?"

"You'll be my daddy?" Hope filled her precious face.

"Yes, honey, I'll be your daddy."

He held her close and wept for the little boy who'd needed a tender daddy instead of the cold floor of an orphanage. And he wept for the little girl who'd now never have to wonder again if someone loved her because she'd have her very own daddy, and he'd love her always.

"Thai, we have to leave." Kinsy's voice was gentle, understanding. When he glanced up at her tear-streaked face, his heart dissolved into a puddle of yearning.

"Run to Aunt Lan. Daddy will be back as soon as he can." He held her tight for a last second, loosened his hold, and she obeyed, running to Lan. *Daddy sure sounded good.*

Thai rose from the step, and Kinsy grabbed his arm. "Stop. This can't wait any longer. I know this is lousy timing, but I've never been good at timing anyway." She glanced at the waiting van. "Thai, I've never apologized—I mean really apologized—for pushing you into this trip." Deep, gut wrenching humility shown in her eyes, reverberated through her words. "I'm so ashamed." A lone tear slid down her cheek. "And so sorry. I didn't really realize until I heard your story—I don't think I would have had the strength to come back."

Thai wrapped his arm around her shoulders and started walking toward the van. "You remember the promise in Romans 8:28? I needed to be on this trip, so God used your bad choice for my good." He stopped dead in his tracks and faced her. "I forgive you, Kinsy." He gently brushed a strand of hair off her cheek.

"Will you kiss her already?" several boys shouted from the van.

A red flush crept up Kinsy's cheeks.

❧

"Would you mind, 'cause I'd really like to take their advice?" Tenderness radiated from Thai's eyes and melted Kinsy's heart. His hand lingered on her shoulder, near her ear. "I wanted to kiss you yesterday by the river, but—okay, I'll be honest—I've wanted to kiss you every day since we got to Vietnam."

"If you kiss me now, I need to know it's because you want to, not because you feel pressured by anyone—especially not by me." She dreamed of nothing more than Thai's kiss, but not with a high price of remorse attached.

"All regrets are behind me. I settled things with God and buried my past here in Vietnam. I'm moving forward." He traced her lips with his thumb. "Will you come with me?"

She barely nodded. Was he saying what she hoped he was? He lowered his head, covering her lips with his in a long, slow kiss. Wolf whistles erupted from the van.

When the kiss ended, he peered into her eyes. "No regrets," he promised. Grabbing her by the waist, he picked her up, and twirled her around. "I love you, Kinsy!" he shouted loud enough for everyone to hear. He stopped twirling and let her down. "I love you!"

The mission team cheered. One of the guys shouted, "You go, Thai!"

"Thai—" She struggled to get the words past the lump in her throat.

"Wait." He gently covered her lips with his fingers. "You need to know, it no longer matters that you're Asian, and I love you more than I ever thought possible. Cherishing you will be the easiest thing I ever do."

Kinsy looked at her beloved through watery eyes. "And I love you, but. . ."

"No, buts. I'm not going to let you get away this time." Thai knelt in the damp grass. Applause broke out in the van.

Kinsy's face grew warm. She laughingly covered it with her hand. "This isn't what I had in mind when I prayed you'd love me with complete abandon."

He only grinned at her. "Kinsy, will you marry me? Not because Cai needs a mother, or for any other reason, but because I can't imagine my life without you. I planned to ask you yesterday down by the river, but things went haywire."

"You planned to ask me yesterday—even after I practically threw myself at your feet and forced you to—"

"You didn't force me into anything. Is that why you ran from me? Because you thought you were pressuring me into—"

"Yes. I just didn't want to make you feel like I was up to my old tricks again. I don't ever again want to push another living soul into anything, especially not you, Thai."

"Well, I had been planning my proposal for weeks. Now will you say yes, so I can get up off this soggy ground?" His eyes danced with pleasure and her heart sang the same tune.

"Yes!"

Rising, he kissed her deeply, passionately. Everyone clapped and cheered, and Cai ran from the orphanage with Lan close on her heels. "Daddy, Daddy!" Cai squealed. "Will Kinsy be my mommy?"

"Yes! Yes she will!" Thai scooped their future daughter into his arms and the three of them shared a family hug, a precursor of things to come.

After Thai and Kinsy exchanged their final good-byes with Cai, they climbed back into the van. There wasn't a dry eye among the participants. As the van pulled away, Thai and Kinsy leaned out the window, waving to Cai.

She smiled and waved back. "Good-bye, Daddy! Good-bye, Mommy," she yelled several times.

When they boarded their airplane, Thai and Kinsy finagled a seat trade with a couple of the kids, so they could sit together on the flight home. "We still have a lot to talk about," Thai whispered.

"It's a long plane ride home," she reminded him.

He shared with her about his mother's death and how he'd blamed himself. He told her about his talks with her birth mother and how she helped him see the truth.

"I might have never found healing if I hadn't come back here and faced my past. I've been fighting a growing love for you since our basketball game last January, and I think you reeled me in at Yosemite. Denying it had nothing to do with you and everything to do with my skewed perception of my mother's death."

"So if a gorgeous blond asked you to marry her—"

"I'd tell her I'm already taken. My heart belongs to a little Vietnamese beauty."

Kinsy leaned over and kissed Thai. She didn't think she'd ever grow tired of his lips.

Being cherished was a sweet feeling. Closing her eyes, she thanked God for the work He'd done in her and in Thai on this trip. She loved the Lord and Thai completely. Victory at last belonged to both of them.

A Letter To Our Readers

Dear Reader:

In order that we might better contribute to your reading enjoyment, we would appreciate your taking a few minutes to respond to the following questions. We welcome your comments and read each form and letter we receive. When completed, please return to the following:

Rebecca Germany, Fiction Editor
Heartsong Presents
PO Box 719
Uhrichsville, Ohio 44683

1. Did you enjoy reading *Remnant of Victory* by Jeri Odell?
   ❑Very much. I would like to see more books by this author!
   ❑Moderately
   I would have enjoyed it more if ________________

   ____

   ____

2. Are you a member of **Heartsong Presents**? Yes ❑ No ❑
   If no, where did you purchase this book?____________

   ____

3. How would you rate, on a scale from 1 (poor) to 5 (superior), the cover design?________________________

4. On a scale from 1 (poor) to 10 (superior), please rate the following elements.

_____ Heroine	_____ Plot
_____ Hero	_____ Inspirational theme
_____ Setting	_____ Secondary characters

5. These characters were special because______________________

____

____

6. How has this book inspired your life?_____________________

____

____

7. What settings would you like to see covered in future **Heartsong Presents** books?___________________________

____

____

8. What are some inspirational themes you would like to see treated in future books?___________________________

____

____

9. Would you be interested in reading other **Heartsong Presents** titles? Yes ❑ No ❑

10. Please check your age range:
    - ❑ Under 18
    - ❑ 18-24
    - ❑ 25-34
    - ❑ 35-45
    - ❑ 46-55
    - ❑ Over 55

11. How many hours per week do you read?___________________

Name ____

Occupation _____________________________________

Address _______________________________________

City ____________________ State ____________ Zip ____________

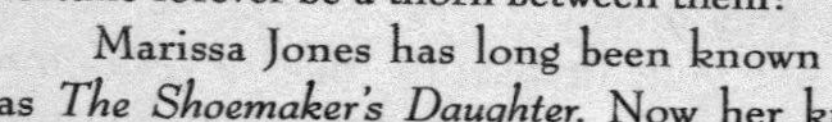